POP-UPS

Contents

2   Getting started
4   Simple pop-ups
6   Pig with stand-out snout
8   Dancing snowmen
10   Floating ghost
12   Gobbling monster
14   Inkblot demon
16   Bat and moon
17   Rocket
18   Cancan pigs
20   Curse of the mummy's tomb
22   Sickly beast
24   Toothy bear
26   House of doom
30   Spinning wheel
31   Templates

Getting started

In this part of the book you can find out how to make all sorts of pop-up cards and other pop-up projects. Step-by-step pictures show you how to make them. Most are simple. Make them for fun, or give them to people on special occassions. Here are some tips to help you before you start.

Things you will need

To make the cards you need these things, plus a few extras, such as paperclips.

Measuring

To make each card in this book, you will need to cut and fold a rectangle of card or paper.

Measurements are given at the top of the page.

All measurements are for cards before they are folded.

10cm (4in)

16cm (6½in)

Before you start each card, turn to the page to see what size rectangle you need to cut.

If it says 10 x 16cm (4 x 6½in), you must cut a card 10cm(4in) wide and 16cm(6½in) long.

Thin card in lots of colours

Thin white paper, such as typing paper

Scissors

Powder and poster paints

Pencil and ruler

Felt tip pens

Paint brushes

Stick of glue

Coloured inks

2

Cutting

Here's how to make sure you cut the edges of the card straight.

Measure from the left-hand edge of the paper, near the top. Make a dot at the right number of centimetres (inches).

Further down the card, measure and mark again.

Draw a line down the card, through the dots. Cut along it to make a straight edge.

Always use a ruler to draw straight lines.

Folding

In this book, two sorts of fold are used a lot.

A mountain fold looks like this.

A valley fold looks like this.

Always fold the longer sides in half.

When you fold a card, press the middle first. Smooth it down with your fingers. Then press outwards from side to side.

Make all folds neatly and press them firmly with your finger and thumb or with a ruler.

Lines you fold are shown like this.

Lines you cut are shown like this.

Decoration

Collect all kinds of bits and bobs to brighten up your pop-ups. These things would be useful.

Pictures cut from magazines

Sequins

Glitter

Scraps of ribbon and lace

Feathers

Wallpaper and wrapping paper

Gold and silver foil

Gold and silver pens (for writing on coloured card)

Finishing touches

Add a picture or a message to the front of the card. Remember to sign it inside, too.

Happy birthday

Congratulations

Be my honey bear

Growl!

Get well soon

Love Billy x

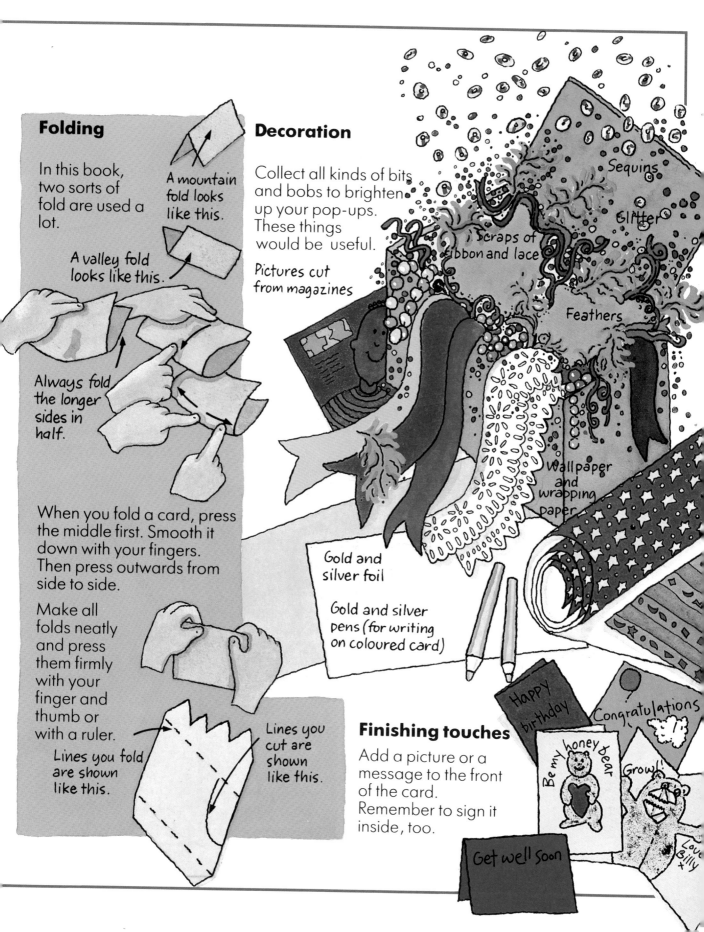

Simple pop-ups

Stand-up card

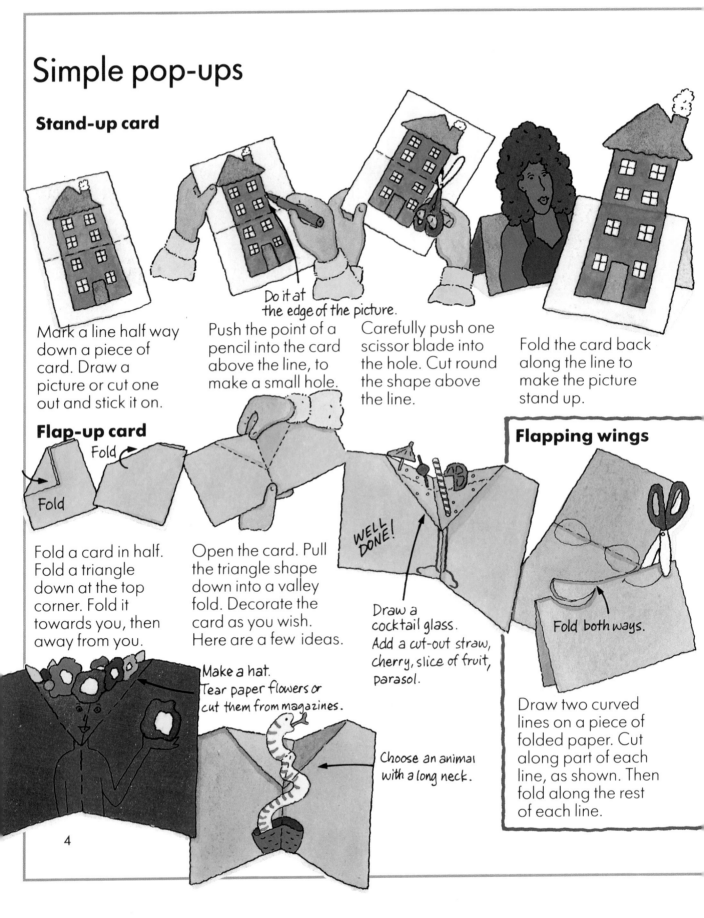

Do it at the edge of the picture.

Mark a line half way down a piece of card. Draw a picture or cut one out and stick it on.

Push the point of a pencil into the card above the line, to make a small hole.

Carefully push one scissor blade into the hole. Cut round the shape above the line.

Fold the card back along the line to make the picture stand up.

Flap-up card

Fold

Fold

Fold a card in half. Fold a triangle down at the top corner. Fold it towards you, then away from you.

Open the card. Pull the triangle shape down into a valley fold. Decorate the card as you wish. Here are a few ideas.

Make a hat. Tear paper flowers or cut them from magazines.

WELL DONE!

Draw a cocktail glass. Add a cut-out straw, cherry, slice of fruit, parasol.

Choose an animal with a long neck.

Flapping wings

Fold both ways.

Draw two curved lines on a piece of folded paper. Cut along part of each line, as shown. Then fold along the rest of each line.

4

Genie in a jar

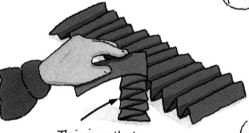

This is called an accordion fold.

You will need an empty plastic jar with a screw-on lid. Mix poster paint and glue and paint inside the jar.

Cut a strip of card three times the height of the jar. Make narrow folds along it (as you would for a fan).

Cut out and colour a genie. Glue it to the top of the folded strip. Stick a feather and some strong thread to the genie's turban.

When you take off the lid, the genie will pop out.

Glue the bottom of the folded strip inside the jar. Tape the end of the thread to the jar lid and screw it on.

BEE HAPPY!

Open the paper and pull the "wings" towards you. Stick the paper onto a card the same size.

Draw a bee's body between the wings. Open and close the card to make the bee's wings flap.

Another idea

Make a single flap as shown, for a newspaper or book.

More ideas

Accordion fold a strip of paper. Glue the ends inside a folded card. The folded strip can be a ballerina's skirt or a clown's ruff.

Pig with stand-out snout

Fold a piece of pink or white card, about 30 x 15cm (12 x 6in). Put it on one side while you make a spring.

To make a spring

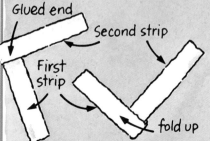

Cut two paper strips, each 1.5 x 15cm (½ x 6in). Dab glue at the end of the first.

Glued end
Second strip
First strip
fold up

Press the second strip on to the glued end at right-angles. Fold the first strip up over the second strip. Carry on folding the strips across each other, until all the paper is used up.

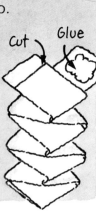

Cut
Glue

Dab some glue under the top flap and press down. Cut off any extra paper to leave a folded square shape.

Inside the card

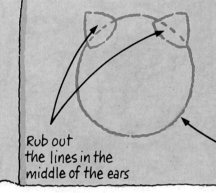

Rub out the lines in the middle of the ears

Draw a pair of feet

Don't use anything to draw round. A wobbly shape is nicer.

Draw a large circle in pencil on the right-hand side, nearer the top than the bottom. Add two ears.

Go over the lines with black felt tip. Glue one end of the spring and press it into the middle of the circle.

To make the snout

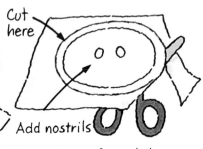

Cut here

Add nostrils

On a piece of card draw a circle in black felt tip. It must be big enough to cover the spring. Cut around the circle outside the line.

Tip

You could give your pig a flower to carry. Make one out of card or cut one from a magazine. Glue the flower between the spring and the snout.

To finish the card

Glue the snout to the top of the spring. The snout will stand out when you open the card.

Draw in the eyes

ON YOUR BIRTHDAY...

MAKE A PIG OF YOURSELF!

Add texture

Dab your pig with a sponge dipped in thick pink paint to give it a mottled look.

Print some straw by dabbing the card with a piece of drinking straw dipped in yellow paint.

Other ideas

Snake pit

Valley fold

Add eyes, nostrils and a tongue

For the snakes' bodies, make three springs of different sizes out of wrapping paper or wallpaper.

Cut a head for each snake. Make a valley fold near the end of each head. Glue the heads to the bodies.

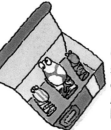

Glue the ends of the snakes' bodies inside a small box with a lid. A teabag box would be ideal.

Glue the back of each head to the box lid. Close the box. When you open it the snakes will rear up.

Boxer

Glue a spring behind the boxing glove

Dancing snowmen

The arms must touch the sides of the paper.

This is an accordion fold.

Fold a piece of white paper, 13 x 30cm (5 x 12in). Fold each side outwards in half again. The edges must line up with the centre fold.

Keeping the paper folded, lightly draw a circle for a snowman's head. Draw an oval for the body. Then add arms, legs and a hat.

Go over the outline with a pencil crayon. Rub out all the other pencil lines.

Fix the snowmen

Fold a piece of black card, 16 x 30cm (6½ x 12in). Put some glue on the backs of the first and last snowmen.

Lay the middle fold of the snowmen along the centre fold of the card. Lay them nearer the top than the bottom of the card.

Press the snowmen down. Pull the two in the middle towards you and close the card. When you open the card, they will stand out.

8

You could draw stars in pencil on the snowman to remind yourself where not to cut.

Make sure the pencil outlines are on the back.

Cut around the outline. Keep the paper folded. Be careful not to cut around the ends of the snowman's arms.

Carefully open out the snowmen. Add faces, scarves and so on. You could make each one different.

Add a snowy lawn

Paint some falling snow

Snip here

Cut a strip of white paper, 4 x 30cm(1½ x 12in). Fold it in the same way as for the snowmen. Snip bumpy shapes in the top.

Glue the lawn to the card in the same way as you glued the snowmen. Leave a space between the snowmen and the lawn.

Other ideas

Draw different Christmas pictures. Each shape must touch the sides of the folded paper.

Christmas trees and stars

Crackers

MERRY   CHRISTMAS

You could make cards like these for other occasions, such as birthdays.

Birthday cakes

Happy   Birthday

Dancing frogs

Floating ghost

Cut two pieces of black card 11 x 19cm(4½ x 7½in). Fold them in half and put one aside.

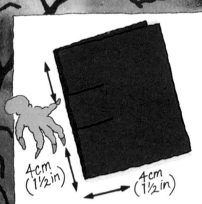

4cm (1½in)

4cm (1½in)

Mountain fold

Make two marks on the folded edge, 4cm(1½in) from each end. Draw two 4cm(1½in) lines from the marks. Cut along them.

Fold the cut middle piece back and press down. Open the flap. Turn the card over and repeat the fold. Open out the flap.

Open the card out. Press the middle piece up from behind into a box shape. Pinch up and crease the centre fold of the box.

Add ghostly noises in silver pen or white paint.

You could stick on a picture cut from a magazine instead.

Cut roughly around the ghost. Then carefully cut it out, leaving a black edge. Turn the ghost over and put some glue near the bottom.

Stick the ghost to the front of the box. It will look as if it is floating against the blackness.

If you make the box smaller, you will have room for a taller ghost.

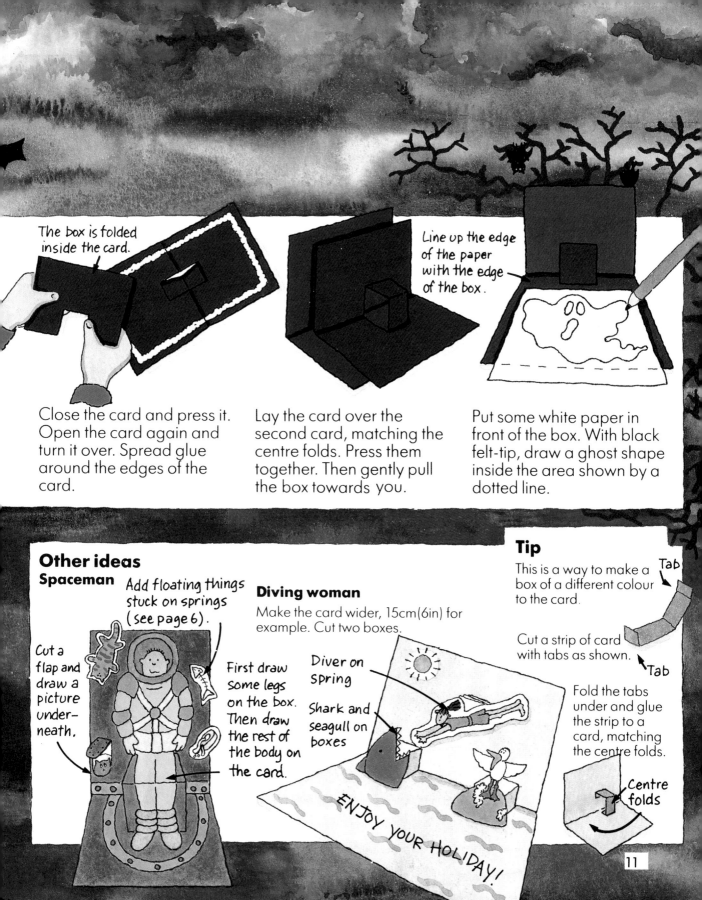

The box is folded inside the card.

Close the card and press it. Open the card again and turn it over. Spread glue around the edges of the card.

Line up the edge of the paper with the edge of the box.

Lay the card over the second card, matching the centre folds. Press them together. Then gently pull the box towards you.

Put some white paper in front of the box. With black felt-tip, draw a ghost shape inside the area shown by a dotted line.

Other ideas

Spaceman

Add floating things stuck on springs (see page 6).

Cut a flap and draw a picture underneath.

Diving woman

Make the card wider, 15cm(6in) for example. Cut two boxes.

First draw some legs on the box. Then draw the rest of the body on the card.

Diver on spring

Shark and seagull on boxes

ENJOY YOUR HOLIDAY!

Tip

This is a way to make a box of a different colour to the card.

Tab

Cut a strip of card with tabs as shown.

Tab

Fold the tabs under and glue the strip to a card, matching the centre folds.

Centre folds

11

Gobbling monster

Fold a piece of red card and one of white paper, each
20 x 28cm(8 x 11in). Put the card aside.

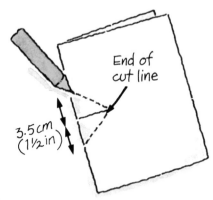

End of
cut line

3.5cm
(1½in)

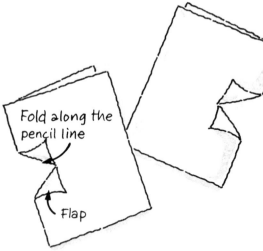

Fold along the
pencil line

Flap

To make the mouth

Mark the folded edge of the
paper 10cm(4in) from the
end. Draw a 5cm(2in) line
from the mark and cut
along it.

Make a mark each side of
the cut line, 3.5cm(1½in)
away from it. Draw a line
from each mark to the end
of the cut line.

Fold back two flaps. Open
out the flaps and turn the
paper over. Fold the flaps
down and then open them
out again.

When you open and
close the card, the
triangles will flap
open and shut, like
a mouth.

Lay the paper out flat. Pinch
up the folds at each end of
the paper. They will change
from valley folds to
mountain folds.

As you pinch them up, push
the folded triangle shapes
through to the other side.
Press the card to flatten the
triangles inside.

Open the red card and put
glue on the outside edges
only. Lay the white paper on
top, matching the centre
folds.

12

Inside the card

Draw a monster around the mouth and colour it. You could make smudgy prints all over it with a small piece of sponge dipped in ink or paint.

COME TO MY PARTY THERE'LL BE LOTS TO EAT

Legs to gobble

4cm (1½in)

1cm (½in)

Draw a line on paper 1cm(½in) from the top. Mark two 4cm(1½in) widths to make tabs and draw some legs below. Cut around the legs and tabs.

Stick on sequins, stars or glitter if you like.

Colour in the legs on both sides. Glue under the tabs and stick them inside the monster's lower jaw so that the legs hang out.

Tip

If you make several invitation cards, accordion fold the paper first. Then you can cut lots of legs out at one time.

Other ideas

Make a jagged cut in the folded paper to look like some teeth.

Stick a 'victim' inside

Add a tongue

Jagged cut

Cut two slits in the folded paper. Rotate the card so that the slits are side by side. Now they can be a cat's eyes or car headlights.

13

Inkblot demon

This makes your demon.

You could add more colours and fold again.

Cut outside the demon's edge.

Cut from the bottom edge of the paper.

1.5cm (¾in)

Drip a few drops of ink or runny paint into the centre of a folded piece of stiff white paper, 13 x 17cm(5 x 6½in).

Close the paper carefully. Press it, to spread the ink out. Open the card and leave it to dry.

Crease the fold the other way, so it changes from a valley fold into a mountain fold. Cut around the demon.

Draw a line across 1.5cm(¾in) from the bottom. Snip the corner off to where the line meets the centre fold.

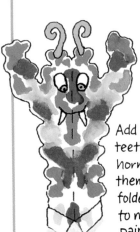

Add eyes, teeth or horns. Cut them from folded paper, to make pairs.

To make the card

5.5 cm (2¼in)

Open the demon out and mountain fold along the lines, to make two tabs. Add eyes, fangs and horns if you like.

Fold a card, 18 x 25cm(7 x 10in). Put a pencil dot on the fold 5.5cms(2¼in) from the top. Draw lines from the dot to the top corners.

Glue the tabs. Put the demon on the pencil dot with the tabs folded behind. Line up each tab along a pencil line and press.

When the glue is dry, fold and press the card. The demon will rear up when you open it again.

14

Add some scenery

Make more inkblots for scenery in front of your demon. Trim them to look like flames, a jungle or a city skyline.

In front of the demon, mark a dot on the fold for the next pop-up. Measure the distance from the dot to the demon.

Measure and mark the same distance from the top corners down each side of the card. Draw lines from the centre dot to the dots on the edges.

Measure the scenery to make sure it will fit in the space. You may need to trim it a bit. Make tabs along the bottom, as before.

Glue here

Glue the tabs along the pencil lines.

Other ideas

Cut the inkblot into a butterfly shape. Stick it on a box (see page 10) or spring (see page 6).

Make a tiny monster. Drip a small blob of paint or ink on paper. Spread it outwards using a straw or the blunt end of a paintbrush.

Tip

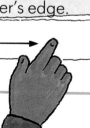

To make long, low scenery, smooth the paint from the fold towards the paper's edge.

When it is dry, stick on cut-out eyes, feet and so on. Mount it on a box or spring.

15

Bat and moon

Trace the bat template on page 32 onto a folded black card, 12 x 24cm (4½ x 9in).

Remember to trace the fold line on the wing.

template on page 32

Tip

If the pencil line does not show up well enough, go over it with a white or yellow pencil crayon.

Do not trace over this line.

Cut the bat out. Fold the wings along the fold lines, first one way, then the other.

Open out the bat, so the centre fold is a mountain fold. Make valley folds on both wings.

Turn the bat over. Put glue between the wing-tips and the wing folds. Turn it over again.

Stick the bat inside a blue card, 15 x 25cm(6 x 10in). Match centre folds. Leave it to dry.

Close the card gently, pulling the centre fold of the bat towards you. Press all over the card.

Cut out a big round or crescent moon. Glue it on the card so that the bat stands out in front of it.

Other ideas

Add a church, a tree or some stars to the background.

Try out different colours for the sky and moon.

Rocket

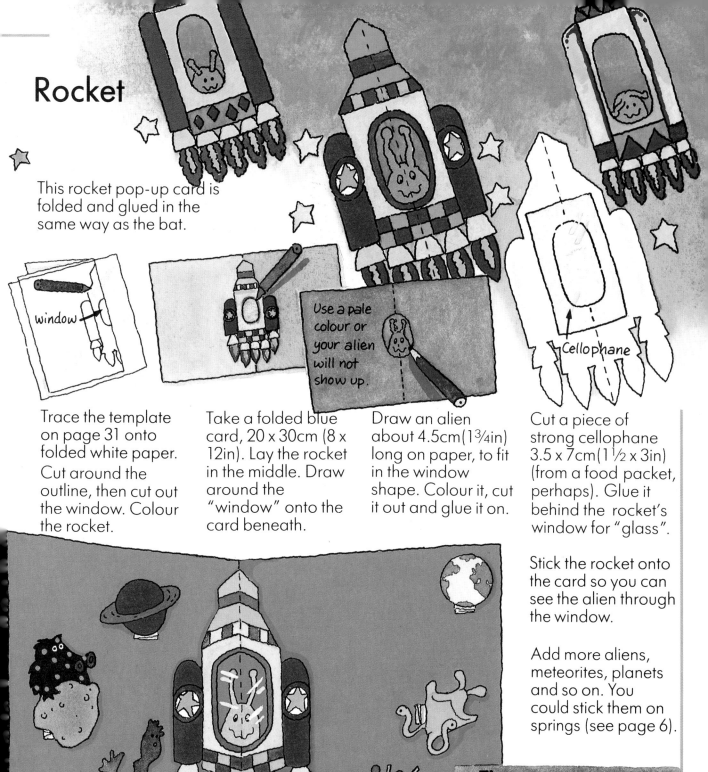

This rocket pop-up card is folded and glued in the same way as the bat.

window

Use a pale colour or your alien will not show up.

Cellophane

Trace the template on page 31 onto folded white paper.

Cut around the outline, then cut out the window. Colour the rocket.

Take a folded blue card, 20 x 30cm (8 x 12in). Lay the rocket in the middle. Draw around the "window" onto the card beneath.

Draw an alien about 4.5cm (1¾in) long on paper, to fit in the window shape. Colour it, cut it out and glue it on.

Cut a piece of strong cellophane 3.5 x 7cm (1½ x 3in) (from a food packet, perhaps). Glue it behind the rocket's window for "glass".

Stick the rocket onto the card so you can see the alien through the window.

Add more aliens, meteorites, planets and so on. You could stick them on springs (see page 6).

Tip
Place extra things so they won't touch each other when you close the card.

Cancan pigs

Fold two bits of pink card, 15 x 16cm(6 x 6½in). On one card draw and cut a box shape (see page 10).

Crease the fold line but do not push the box through. Mark off the box into six equal strips for legs.

Each strip is 1.5cm (¾in) wide.

Cut along the lines. Open the card and push the box shape through.

Smooth the card out flat. Draw and colour a foot at the end of each leg.

Inside the card

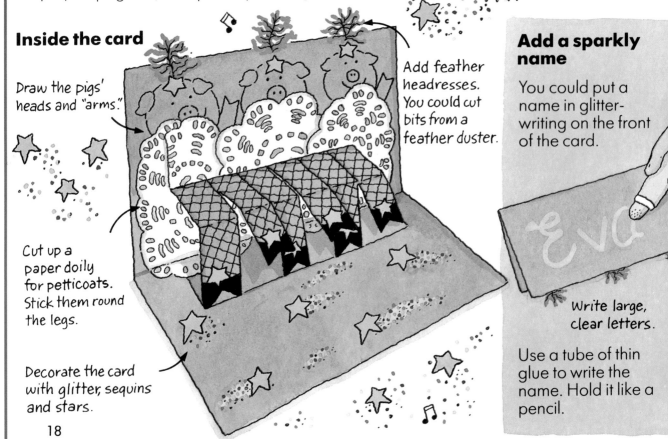

Draw the pigs' heads and "arms."

Cut up a paper doily for petticoats. Stick them round the legs.

Decorate the card with glitter, sequins and stars.

Add feather headresses. You could cut bits from a feather duster.

Add a sparkly name

You could put a name in glitter-writing on the front of the card.

Write large, clear letters.

Use a tube of thin glue to write the name. Hold it like a pencil.

18

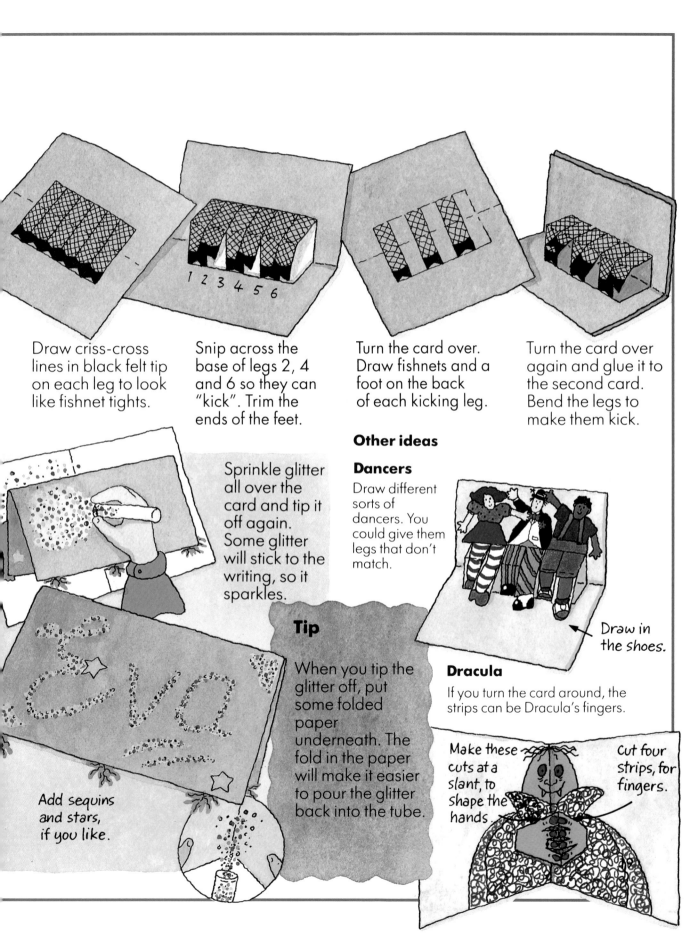

Draw criss-cross lines in black felt tip on each leg to look like fishnet tights.

Snip across the base of legs 2, 4 and 6 so they can "kick". Trim the ends of the feet.

1 2 3 4 5 6

Turn the card over. Draw fishnets and a foot on the back of each kicking leg.

Turn the card over again and glue it to the second card. Bend the legs to make them kick.

Sprinkle glitter all over the card and tip it off again. Some glitter will stick to the writing, so it sparkles.

Add sequins and stars, if you like.

Tip

When you tip the glitter off, put some folded paper underneath. The fold in the paper will make it easier to pour the glitter back into the tube.

Other ideas

Dancers

Draw different sorts of dancers. You could give them legs that don't match.

Draw in the shoes.

Dracula

If you turn the card around, the strips can be Dracula's fingers.

Make these cuts at a slant, to shape the hands

Cut four strips, for fingers.

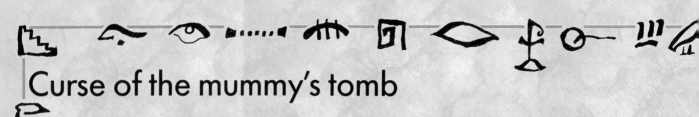

Curse of the mummy's tomb

Take a piece of coloured card, 15 x 21cm (6 x 8½in). Fold it in half lengthways to make a tall, thin card. Trace the mummy's tomb template on page 32.

Cut strips from the folded edge straight across towards the middle. End each cut at the outline of the mummy.

Make the strips as thin as you can.

Outline of mummy

Tip

If you are worried about cutting straight, draw the lines first with a pencil and ruler.

Make sure all the strips go through to the other side.

Unfold the strips again and smooth them flat. Very carefully open the paper out flat. Pinch up the ends and press the strips through to the other side.

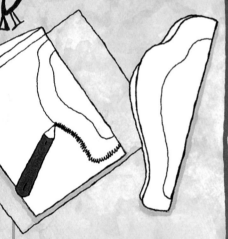

Fold a piece of white paper. Trace the shape onto the paper. Go over the lines with black felt tip. Then cut around the shape.

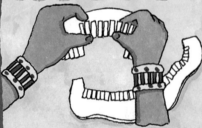

Fold the strips back along the outline. Fold a few at a time, starting with the ones in the middle. Unfold the strips. Turn the paper over and fold them again.

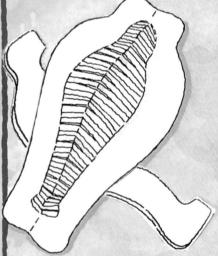

Fold the paper and press the strips flat. Open the paper out to see the mummy wrapped in bandages.

To decorate the mummy

Draw a line 0.5cm(¼in) from the edge all the way around, as a margin. Colour the margin brown, for the mummy's wooden tomb (called the sarcophagus).

Use dark paint to fill in between the margin and the mummy, to make it look dark inside the sarcophagus.

Draw hieroglyphics (Egyptian picture symbols) inside the sarcophagus. Look in books about Ancient Egypt for ideas.

To finish the card

Put glue on the back of the sarcophagus and stick it to the blue card, matching the centre folds.

On the front of the card draw some more Egyptian things, such as pyramids or gods.

Gold or silver pen would show up well against the dark background.

Another idea
Knight in armour

Make a shorter, wider paper shape for a knight's head and body. Glue it to the top half of a card.

Cut wider strips, to look like armour.

Add arms, legs, a shield and a sword.

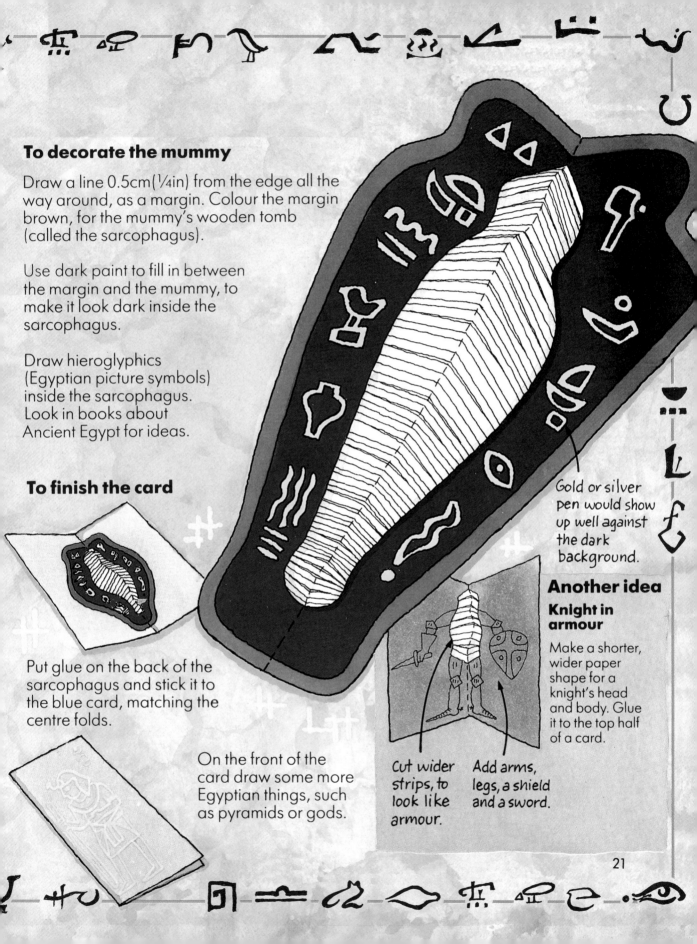

Sickly beast

Fold two pieces of white or pale-coloured paper, 15 x 28cm(6 x 11in).

Make a pair of beast's eyes

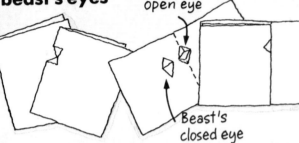

Beast's open eye

Beast's closed eye

Draw a sickly beast

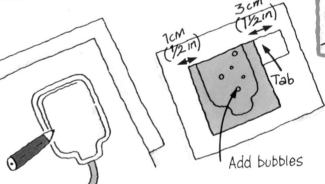

Draw a tube going from the beast to the bottle.

Mark 5cm(2in) down the folded edge of one card. Make a 1.5cm(½in) cut. Fold back two flaps. Then fold them inside the card (see page 12).

Next to the "eye", draw a matching diamond shape to look like a closed eye. Close the card and put it on top of the other open card.

On the top card, draw a beast in a hospital bed. Draw a bottle for blood 2cm (¾in) from the top and 2cm(¾in) from the edge of the card. Cut out the bottle shape.

Fill the bottle with beastly blood

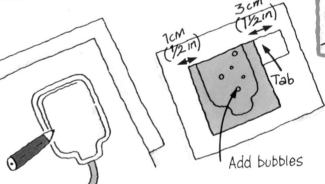

1cm (½in)

3cm (1½in)

Tab

Add bubbles

Draw along the edges of the V shape to make a V on the lower card. Then draw another V so it now makes a diamond.

Lift off the top card. Colour the diamond to look like an eyeball. Spread the colour over the edges of the diamond too.

Lay the beast card over a piece of stiff white paper. Draw around inside the bottle shape. Lift off the card.

Add 1cm around the shape, and a 3cm(1½in) tab. Colour it green (but not the tab) and cut it out.

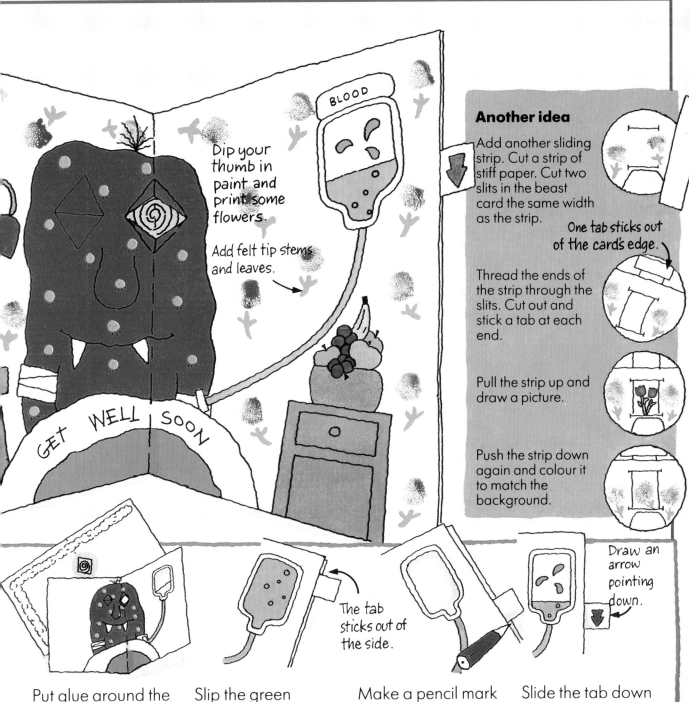

Dip your thumb in paint and print some flowers.

Add felt tip stems and leaves.

BLOOD

Another idea

Add another sliding strip. Cut a strip of stiff paper. Cut two slits in the beast card the same width as the strip.

One tab sticks out of the card's edge.

Thread the ends of the strip through the slits. Cut out and stick a tab at each end.

Pull the strip up and draw a picture.

Push the strip down again and colour it to match the background.

GET WELL SOON

The tab sticks out of the side.

Draw an arrow pointing down.

Put glue around the top, bottom and left-hand edge of the backing card. Stick the beast card on top.

Slip the green shape inside the card so the bottle is full. Slide it down gently until the bottle looks empty.

Make a pencil mark below the tab and slide it up again. Glue up the side of the card, as far as the mark.

Slide the tab down and draw splashes on the card behind. Slide the tab up and down to fill and empty the bottle.

Toothy bear

Make some snapping jaws

Fold a piece of brown or yellow card 21 x 28cm(8 x 11in).

Mark the fold, 6cm (2½in) from the top and 7cm(3in) from the bottom.

Take two smaller bits of the same coloured card and fold them.

Trace the bear's jaw templates on page 32 onto the cards. Cut them out.

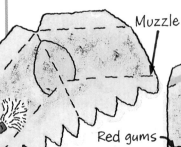

Muzzle

Red gums

Paint the bear's muzzle with a nearly dry brush and black paint.

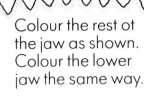

Black nose

White teeth

Colour the rest ot the jaw as shown. Colour the lower jaw the same way.

Put glue on the upper jaw tabs Fold them behind as mountain folds.

Place the point where the tabs meet onto the upper mark on the folded card.

Tip

You may find it easier to press one tab into place, then the other.

Valley folds

Press the centre folds in the jaw and nose into valley folds.

Fold the card and press it. Open it and stick the lower jaw in the same way.

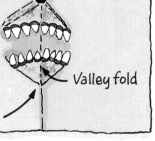

Match the middle of the tabs to the lower mark.

Valley fold

Pull out the jaw. Press the centre fold in the lower jaw to make a valley fold.

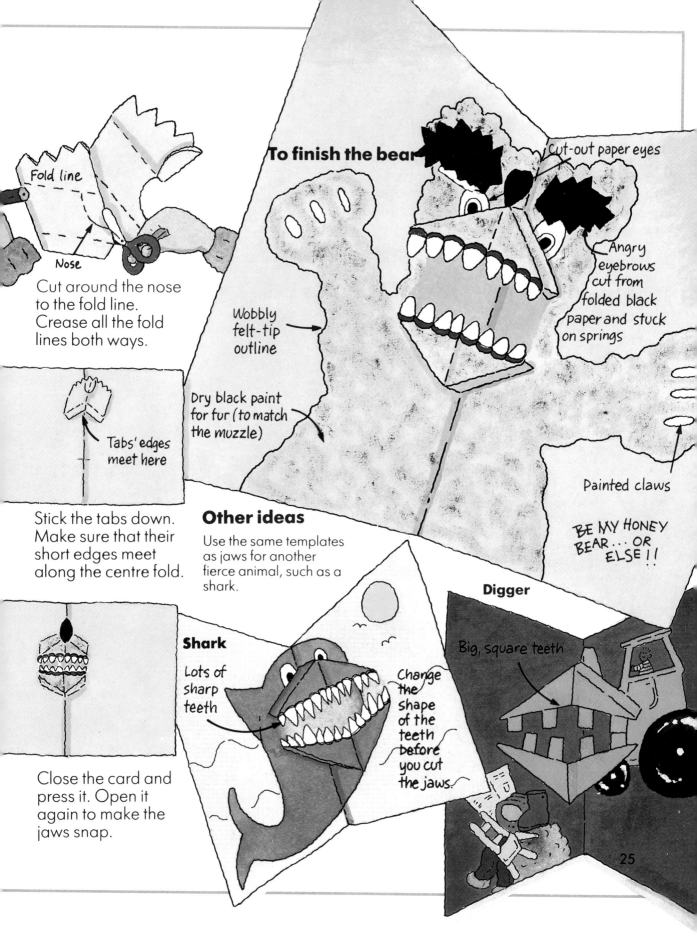

Fold line

Nose

Cut around the nose to the fold line. Crease all the fold lines both ways.

Tabs' edges meet here

Stick the tabs down. Make sure that their short edges meet along the centre fold.

Close the card and press it. Open it again to make the jaws snap.

To finish the bear

Cut-out paper eyes

Wobbly felt-tip outline

Dry black paint for fur (to match the muzzle)

Angry eyebrows cut from folded black paper and stuck on springs

Painted claws

BE MY HONEY BEAR... OR ELSE!!

Other ideas

Use the same templates as jaws for another fierce animal, such as a shark.

Shark

Lots of sharp teeth

Change the shape of the teeth before you cut the jaws.

Digger

Big, square teeth

25

House of doom

This scary scene uses lots of pop-ups. On the next four pages you can find out how to make some of them. You can see how to make the rest by looking back to the page numbers given. You do not have to make all these pop-ups. You could add some of your own instead.

Spook

Twisted branches

Tumble-down walls

The background

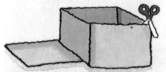

Cut the top and one side off a large box. Choose one made of thin card, so it is easy to cut.

Line the box with coloured paper. Paint a spooky black background and floor.

Trim off the edges and corners to make jagged turret and tree shapes.

Rat in a cage

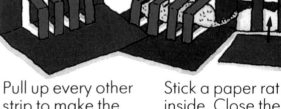

Make a card with a box fold in it (see page 18). Cut thin strips to the fold line. Open the card.

Pull up every other strip to make the bars of the cage. Glue one side to the floor of the box.

Stick a paper rat inside. Close the card and stick extra paper on the top to hide the rat.

Clock striking midnight

Bat and moon

Stick a moon on the background. Make a bat and glue its wing-tips so it overlaps the moon.

Flapping owl (page 4)

Stick a cut-out owl on a flap-up card. Add fierce-looking eyes .

Mummy (page 20)

Cut a door out of paper and glue a mummy inside. Paint around and behind the mummy with black paint.

Colourful spook (page 14)

Make a card with a box fold. Cut one end into a curved door shape. Make an inkblot spook and stick it onto the box.

To close the pop-ups

Glue the pop-ups inside the box. Make sure you stick them so they open out the right way.

Using a ball point pen, make a small hole near the open edge of each pop-up.

Poke paper fasteners through from behind each hole. Open them out to hold the doors shut.

Tree with blinking eyes

Snip the top of the paper into branch shapes.

Paint a tree trunk inside the box. Stick some red paper onto it. Cut a piece of black paper big enough to cover it.

Cut eyeholes near the bottom of the black paper. Put glue along the sides and bottom. Stick it over the red paper.

Leave the top edge unglued. A pair of red eyes should show through the eyeholes. Draw in the eyeballs.

Slide a long piece of black paper into the paper "pocket". Move it up and down to make the eyes open and close.

27

Beckoning hand

Tab
Fold line

On a piece of folded paper draw a nightgown sleeve. with a tab at the end. Draw in a fold line as shown. Cut the sleeve out.

Bend the sleeve both ways along the fold line. Cut a door from folded black card. Put glue on the tab. Stick the sleeve near the bottom of the door.

Bend the sleeve along the fold line, so it lifts when you open the door. Colour the tab black. Stick the door inside the box.

Cut out and stick a ghostly hand inside the sleeve edge nearest to you. When you open and close the door, the hand will beckon.

Snake

Draw a spiral shape. Start in the middle and work outwards. Draw snake patterns, eyes and nostrils.

Cut around the edge. Then cut in towards the middle, following the line of the spiral.

Make a trap door

Draw a circle on folded paper and cut it out. Leave an uncut "hinge" at the folded edge.

Glue behind head

Glue under tail

Glue each end of the snake to one half of the trap door. Stick the trap to the floor of the box.

Skeleton

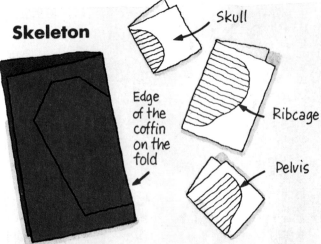

Skull

Edge of the coffin on the fold

Ribcage

Pelvis

Draw a coffin on folded black paper and cut it out.

Cut skeleton shapes, using the mummy technique (page 20).

High-rise ghost

Slit

Cut the top off a small box. Paint it black. Cut a slit at the back, from the top almost to the bottom.

Hold the box in position inside the large box and draw around it. Cut a matching slit in the large box, as shown.

Put sticky tape at the top to seal the slit. Glue the small box in place so that the slits line up.

To make the ghost

Accordion fold a strip of paper. Stick a cut-out ghost on the top (see page 5).

Add arms on springs

Cut a strip of stiff card. Cut a slit at one end. Bend the ends opposite ways.

Glue the ends to the back of the ghost. Thread the card strip through the slit in the box.

Stick the end of the folded paper strip to the floor of the turret.

Slide the card strip up to make the ghost pop up.

Other ideas

Instead of a box you could make a pop-up book.

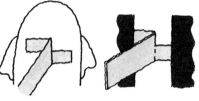

Make several pop-up cards of the same size. Stick them back-to-back to make a book.

Write a ghost story for your book. You could use gold or silver pen to write out the words.

Try out different ideas for stories with other sorts of pop-ups.

Black paint around skeleton

Paint arm and leg bones

Glue the skeleton inside the coffin, matching the folds.

Spinning wheel

Fold in half.

Fold again.

This is the middle of the wheel.

Put a jar lid on a piece of card so that it overlaps the edge. Draw around it.

Draw around the lid twice more on paper and cut out two wheel shapes.

Fold one wheel in four. Lay it over the other wheel and make a mark by the point.

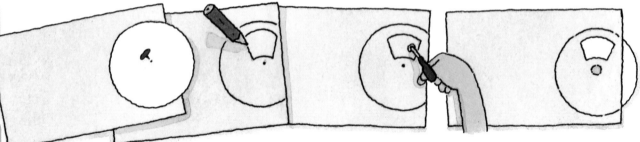

Put the open wheel over the circle on the card. Push a pin through the middle to make a hole in the circle.

Inside the circle draw a window above the pinhole and cut it out.

Put the wheel under the card and push a paper fastener through both pinholes.

Open out the fastener. Spin the wheel to make sure it moves freely.

Rub out the pencil circle. Fold the card and draw a picture around the window.

Draw more pictures through the window onto the wheel, turning as you go.

You could add a spinning wheel to a pop-up card.

Templates

To make some of the cards in this book, you need to trace the templates (outline shapes) on this page and the next.

How to trace a template

Keep the paper in place with paperclips.

Use a ruler to help you trace the straight lines.

Lay a piece of tracing (or greaseproof) paper over the template you want to trace. Trace the outline with a pencil.

Unclip the tracing and turn it over. Cover the outline very thickly with a soft pencil. Turn the tracing over again.

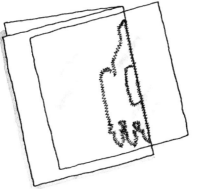

Lay the tracing on top of a folded card. Line up the right-hand side of the traced shape with the folded edge of the card.

Go over the traced outline again using a sharp pencil or ball point pen. Press hard so a line appears on the paper beneath.

Rocket

window

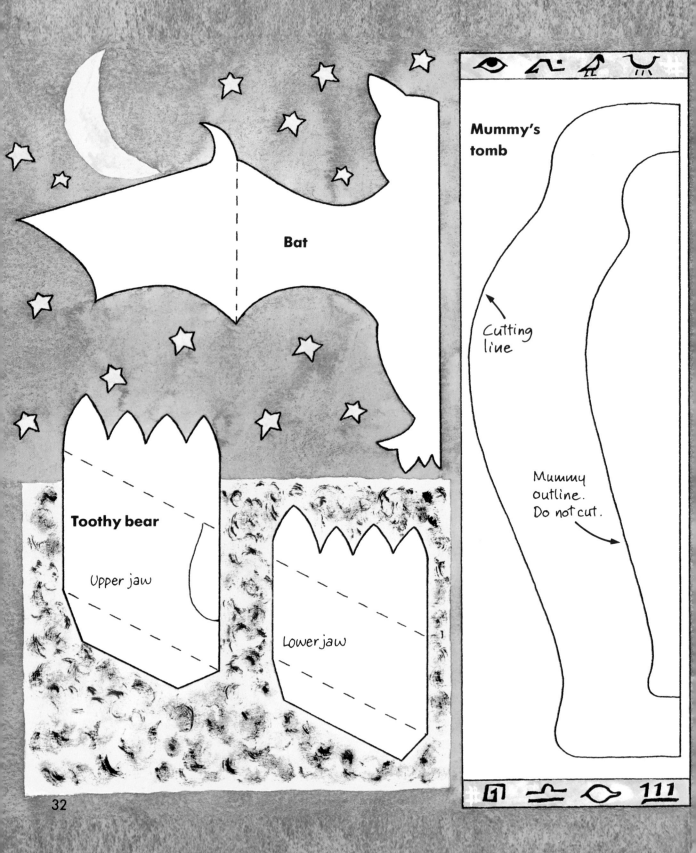

Bat

Mummy's tomb

Cutting line

Mummy outline. Do not cut.

Toothy bear

Upper jaw

Lower jaw

ORIGAMI

Origami consultant:
Sarah Goodall

With special thanks to: Wendy Ball,
Debbie Collins, Marissa Goodman,
John Humphrey, Matthew Jones,
Hannah Mander, David Milligan,
Laura Parsons and John Stapleton.

Contents

34   What is origami?

36   Quick and easy boxes

38   Party hats

40   Flutter butterfly and Space spinner

42   Viking boat and snapping dragon

44   Big bang

46   Fearsome fangs

48   Jumping frog

50   Bombs away

52   Finger puppets

54   Jewellery

56   Flapping bird

58   Starbox

60   Lily

62   Stacking tree

64   Tricky folds

What is origami?

'Origami' is a Japanese word which means 'paper folding'. Hundreds of years ago, when paper was first invented, the Japanese folded it into dolls and flowers for special ceremonies. Now that paper is cheap and plentiful lots of people fold paper just for fun.

This part of the book teaches you how to make lots of origami toys and decorations. It starts off with simple models and gets harder as you go along. Make sure you start at the beginning. Models marked ☆ are the easy ones; models marked ☆☆☆ are the hardest. The tips on these pages will help you before you start.

What sort of paper?

Any paper that folds well is good for origami. Traditional origami paper is coloured on one side. Models are invented so that some bits are white and other bits are coloured.

You can buy packs of coloured squares from good toy departments and Japanese shops. Or you can order them from the British Origami Society (see page 64 for the address).

Useful types of paper

Wrapping paper is good because it has a plain and a coloured side.

Tissue paper is useful for small, delicate models.

You can even use pages from an old magazine, bus tickets or any small piece of paper.

Writing paper folds well and is strong.

Newspaper is handy for big models.

Silver and gold foil paper looks good.

Very thin cardboard is extra strong but harder to fold.

You could paint your own paper.

Symbols

Sometimes symbols are used to help you follow each step. These are the main ones:

Turn the paper over.

Turn the paper around.

Fold and then unfold the paper to make a crease.

To make a square

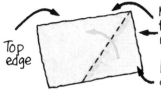

Top edge

Make sure these edges meet.

Bottom corner

A lot of origami models start with a square. Make a square from an oblong as above.

Folding tips

You will learn lots of different folds through the book. The difficult ones are listed on page 64. The picture opposite shows you how to fold neatly. Below it are three good tips to remember.

- - - - Valley fold.

- · - · - Mountain fold.

This is a valley fold.

This is a mountain fold.

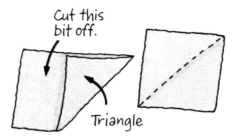

Cut this bit off.

Triangle

Fold the bottom corner up to the top edge to make a triangle.

Hold the corners together.

Press down in the middle first.

Smooth to the side.

1. Always fold neatly, making sure the corners and edges meet. It is easier to be accurate if you fold away from you.

2. Work on a hard surface and press firmly along each fold.

3. Check the picture after every step to see if your paper looks the same.

Cut along the side of the triangle you just made. Open out the paper to see your square.

TRICKY

Some folds are hard the first time you try them. Watch out for the 'tricky' warnings which mark the most difficult bits. If you get stuck fold something else and then try again later.

Tip

Small origami models often look best, but big ones are easier to fold. Start a new model with a big square. When you can fold it easily, use a small one.

To find the middle of a square

Fold the paper in half from side to side. Then unfold it.

Then fold it in half from top to bottom and unfold it.

The middle is where the creases meet.

The middle

To find the middle of an edge

Pinch here.

Fold the corners together and pinch in the middle. Unfold it.

This is the middle.

The pinch mark is the middle.

Quick and easy boxes

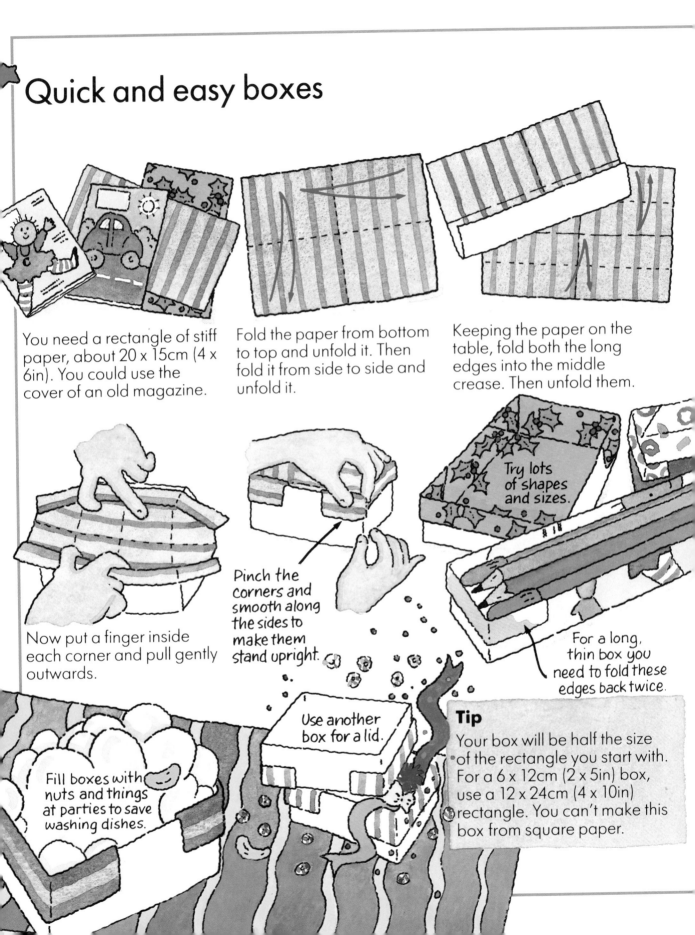

You need a rectangle of stiff paper, about 20 x 15cm (4 x 6in). You could use the cover of an old magazine.

Fold the paper from bottom to top and unfold it. Then fold it from side to side and unfold it.

Keeping the paper on the table, fold both the long edges into the middle crease. Then unfold them.

Try lots of shapes and sizes.

Now put a finger inside each corner and pull gently outwards.

Pinch the corners and smooth along the sides to make them stand upright.

For a long, thin box you need to fold these edges back twice.

Fill boxes with nuts and things at parties to save washing dishes.

Use another box for a lid.

Tip
Your box will be half the size of the rectangle you start with. For a 6 x 12cm (2 x 5in) box, use a 12 x 24cm (4 x 10in) rectangle. You can't make this box from square paper.

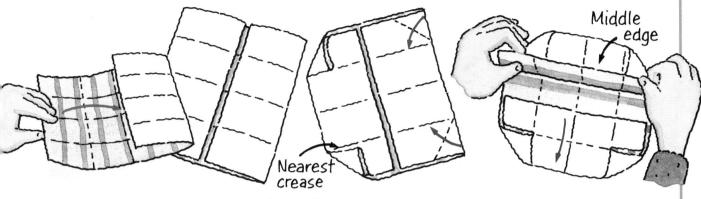

Fold both the short edges into the middle crease and leave them there.

Fold in all the corners so that they meet the nearest crease, as shown here.

Fold back the edges in the middle so that they cover the corners.

Other ideas

Gift boxes

Match the edges carefully.

Glue the white sides together.

You could cut out a rectangle afterwards.

Stick two pieces of coloured wrapping paper together.

Allow the paper to dry before you start folding it.

Pack your box with a face cloth, soap and bath pearls. Or fill it with sweets or nuts.

Wrap it in cling film and tie on a ribbon. Add a paper flower for decoration (see page 60).

Nest of boxes

Prepare several paper rectangles. Make the sides of each one 2cm (1in) smaller than the one before.

10 x 16 cm (3 x 6 in)

12 x 18 cm (4 x 7 in)

14 x 20 cm (5 x 8 in)

Stack them inside each other when empty and then use them to hold things such as buttons or paper clips.

Basket

Cut a long strip of paper. Fold the long edges into the middle.

Then fold it in half lengthways.

Stick one end to each side of a box.

Fill it with origami flowers (see page 60).

Party hats

To make hats that fit you need large squares. Wrapping paper is good. Or use newspaper and paint one side.

Pill box hat

Take a 40cm (12in) square of paper and label the corners in red and blue pen on both sides, as shown.

With the white side up, fold the blue corners together.

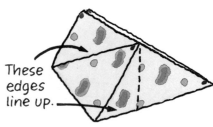

These edges line up.

Fold one red corner across to the opposite side so that the top and bottom edges line up.

These edges meet.

Fold the other red corner across in the same way. Check that the edges meet.

This is the other side.

Fold the top blue corner up over the edges. Turn the paper over and do the same again.

Stick a gift bow to the front and tuck a feather in the back.

Other ideas
Bird mask

Leave the last corner, on the side with no folds, pointing down to make the beak. Paint it yellow.

Cut out nostrils so you can see through the holes.

Tape some feathers to the top for plumage.

Draw on big eyes.

Clown hat

Make a crepe paper fringe for the hair.

Stick a paper flower on the front.

To make the fringe

Use a strip of crepe paper about 15 x 30cm (6 x 12in). Make lots of cuts along one edge.

Glue the other edge inside the rim of your hat. Remember to leave a space for your face.

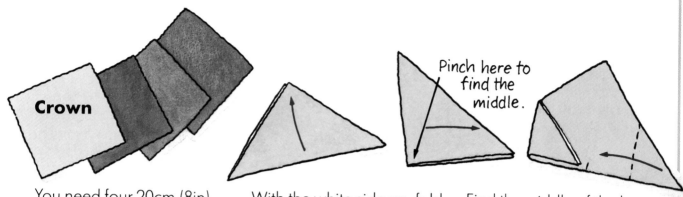

Crown

You need four 20cm (8in) squares of paper. Take one square and turn it so that one corner is towards you.

With the white side up, fold the bottom corner to the top corner.

Pinch here to find the middle.

Find the middle of the long edge by folding it in half. Then fold the side corners into the middle.

Fold all your squares in the same way. Then stand them in a square with the corners pointing inwards, ready to join together.

Make these folds meet.

To link them together slot each corner inside the one next to it, making sure that the folds meet.

Other ideas

Crown of jewels

Stick on gum drops or brightly-coloured buttons as jewels.

Or crumple up tinfoil and cover it with transparent, coloured wrappers.

Rich gold crown

Use paper that is coloured on both sides. Stick gold doilies to one side. Trim off any overlapping bits. Fold each square with the doily side down.

Bend the inner points into the centre and tape them together.

You could turn down the top corner to make a white diamond pattern.

Add some tape to make the corners stronger.

Use more squares to make a bigger crown.

Bend these two first.

Stick a jewel in the middle.

Flutter butterfly

This butterfly is very easy to fold and it flutters through the air when you throw it

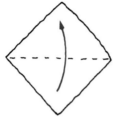

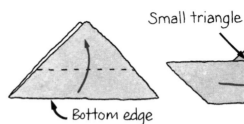

Small triangle

Bottom edge

Use a square of shiny paper for the best effect. Or paint on your own splatter design, as shown below.

Turn the paper so that one corner is towards you, white side up. Then fold the bottom corner to the top.

Fold up the bottom edge, leaving a small triangle peeping out at the top.

Fold the paper in half from side to side. Make sure all the edges meet.

Fold the top layer only here.

These are the wings.

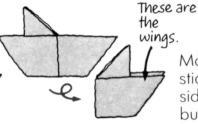

It tumbles...

Fold back the top layer along the dotted line marked in the picture.

Turn the paper over and fold the other side in exactly the same way.

Make the wings stick out to the side. Hold the butterfly beneath them and throw it gently forwards.

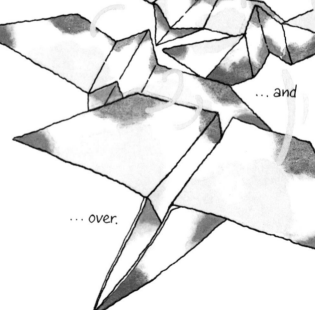

... over

... and

... over.

To paint a splatter design

Make sure you have some newspaper underneath.

Fold the square in half diagonally. Then unfold it.

Splash some paint on one half of the paper only.

Start folding with the crease vertical like this.

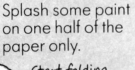

Fold it in half and press down hard.

Unfold the paper and leave it to dry.

40

Space spinner

You need eight small squares of coloured paper. Use fluorescent or shiny paper for a really bright effect.

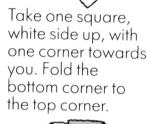

Take one square, white side up, with one corner towards you. Fold the bottom corner to the top corner.

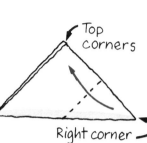

Top corners

Right corner

Fold the right corner up to the top corners to make a small triangle.

Small triangle

Fold all the other squares in exactly the same way. Then join them together as shown below.

Push here to open the triangle.

Triangle

Pointed end

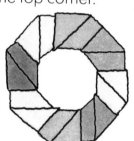

Slot the pointed end of each piece of paper inside the small triangle of the next one.

Keep joining them until you have a complete circle. Then turn the space spinner over.

Fold the top one only.

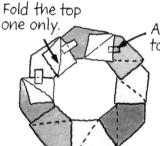

Add tape to secure.

Fold back the top flap on each section so that it sticks up in the air.

Throw it flat, like a frisbee, to make it spin through the air.

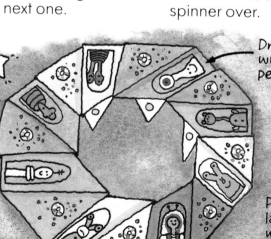

Draw on windows with aliens peeping out.

Paint on landing lights with fluorescent pen.

Viking ship and snapping dragon

Both these models use the same folds to begin with. Start by doing the steps below.

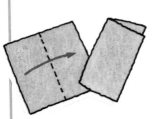

Use a square of strong paper such as writing paper or brown wrapping paper. Fold it in half from side to side.

Fold the right edge back to meet the folded edge.

Turn the paper over. Fold the right edge back to the folded edge. Then unfold it.

Fold all the corners into the middle crease.

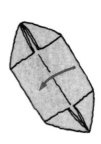

Fold the right edge back to the folded edge again. Now you can make the viking ship or the snapping dragon.

Viking ship

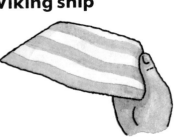

Hold the paper as shown here. Put your fingers inside and your thumb ½cm (¼in) from the top of the side fold.

With your other hand, push the corner over your thumbnail. Squash it down flat.

Fold the other corner in the same way.

Add a coin to balance it.

Turn the boat over and float it. It will sail best with something inside.

To make the mast and sail

Press some playdough in the bottom of the boat. Stick a drinking straw into it for the mast.

Snapping dragon

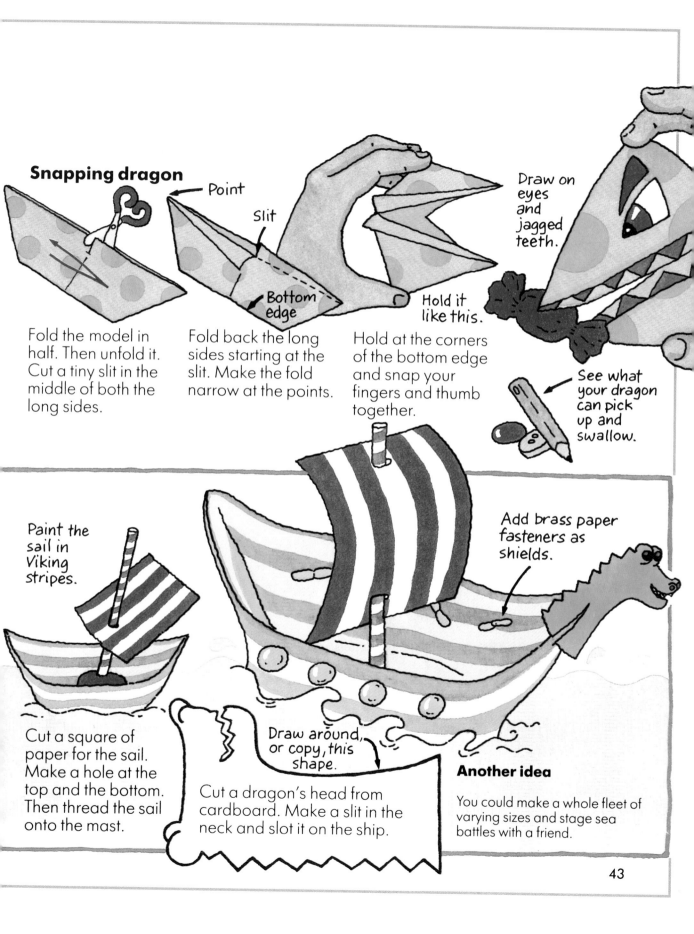

Point

Slit

Bottom edge

Fold the model in half. Then unfold it. Cut a tiny slit in the middle of both the long sides.

Fold back the long sides starting at the slit. Make the fold narrow at the points.

Hold it like this.

Hold at the corners of the bottom edge and snap your fingers and thumb together.

Draw on eyes and jagged teeth.

See what your dragon can pick up and swallow.

Paint the sail in Viking stripes.

Add brass paper fasteners as shields.

Cut a square of paper for the sail. Make a hole at the top and the bottom. Then thread the sail onto the mast.

Draw around, or copy, this shape.

Cut a dragon's head from cardboard. Make a slit in the neck and slot it on the ship.

Another idea

You could make a whole fleet of varying sizes and stage sea battles with a friend.

43

★ Big bang

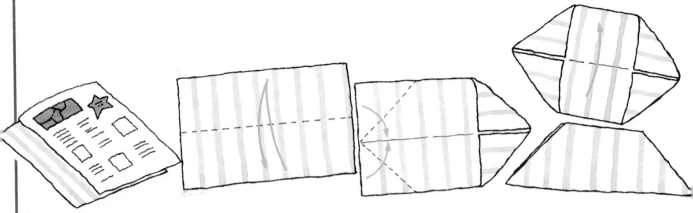

Take a large rectangle of thin paper. A sheet of newspaper or thin brown wrapping paper makes a good loud noise.

Fold the longest sides of the paper together. Then unfold them.

Fold down each corner, matching one side with the middle crease.

Fold the paper in half along the middle crease.

Middle crease   **Bottom edge**

Fold the paper in half again from side to side. Then unfold it.

Fold up the bottom corners so that the bottom edge meets the middle crease. Turn the paper over.

Make sure it looks like this.   Hold this end.

Have this edge towards you.

Fold it in half from side to side. Pick up the banger and hold it firmly at the open end.

Make sure the long edge is towards you. Then put your hand in the air and bring it down sharply. The paper will open with a bang.

Other ideas

Try a 'quick on the draw' contest. See who can make the first bang after a count of three.

Or stand back to back with a friend, walk five paces away from each other, then see who can turn and draw first. Try a banger in each hand for double-barrelled draws.

Customize your banger

Try making bigger and smaller bangers. Each size makes a different noise.

Paint on different words and designs.

Stick on silver lightning flashes.

You could draw on clouds.

write on noisy words.

Add glitter and sequins.

ZAP!

CRACK!

ZOOM

Add stars.

BANG!

Snowstorm

Tear up lots of small pieces of paper and tuck them inside the fold. When the banger snaps open the "snow" will scatter all over your victim.

Be prepared to clear up afterwards.

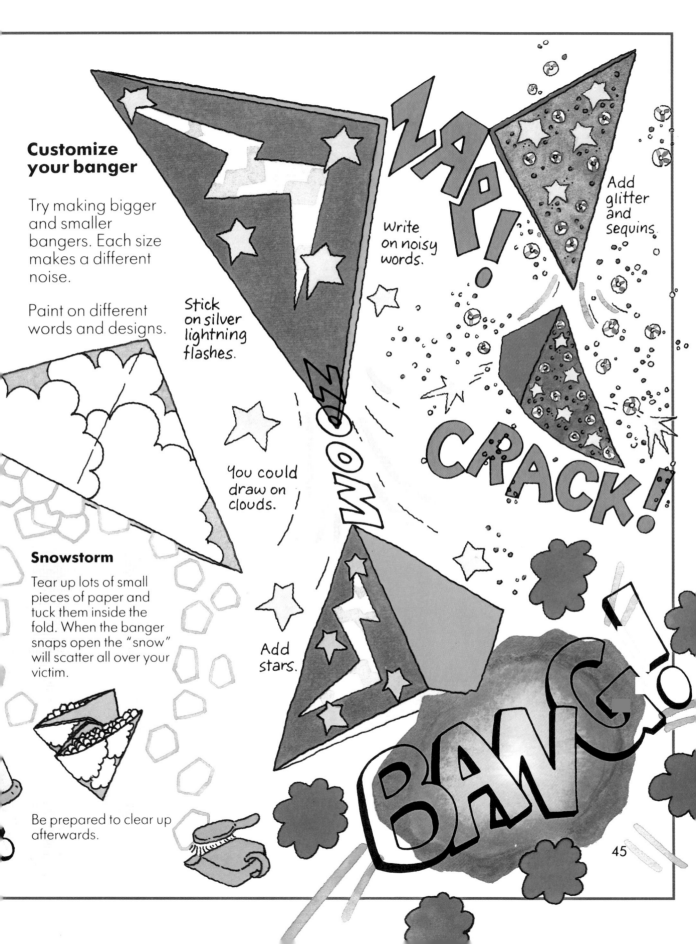

45

Fearsome fangs

Use a rectangle of paper twice as long as it is wide, for example, 8 x 16cm (3 x 6 in). Colour one side bright red for the lips.

Leave the other side white for the fangs. Label the corners green and blue on both sides as shown in the first picture.

Fold this edge.

With the white side up, fold the paper in half from side to side. Unfold it.

Fold it in half from top to bottom and then unfold it again.

Fold the green corners and the blue corners into the middle crease.

Fold the left edge into the middle again, to cover the green corners.

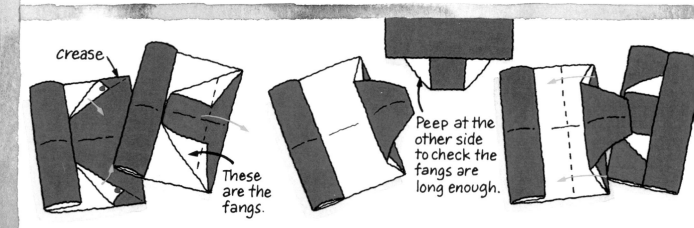

crease

These are the fangs.

Peep at the other side to check the fangs are long enough.

Check that your paper looks like the first picture above, then fold in again along the crease.

Fold the fangs out to the side so that they stick out over the edge.

Fold the right side into the middle so that the red lips meet and the white fangs stick out.

The blue corners almost touch the middle crease like this.

TRICKY

Fold the blue corners towards the middle, bending along the dotted line shown in the picture.

Check that your paper looks like the picture above, then unfold the corners.

Now fold the blue corners in to meet the crease you just made.

Tip

Hold the edges of the mouth between your thumbs and fingers. Use your first fingers to smooth out the fold.

TRICKY

Turn the paper over and fold in all the corners.

Shape the lips by gently denting the folds at the top and bottom.

To open and close the mouth, hold it at the corners and squeeze gently.

Other ideas

You could stick your fangs onto party invitations or balloons for hallowe'en.

Come to my party ...

... if you dare!

Draw on a face.

Make a smaller mouth to fit in your hand. Curve your thumb and first finger around it. Paint fierce eyes on your finger and squeeze gently to make the mouth talk.

Jumping frog

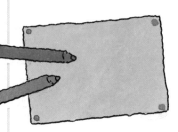

Take a rectangle of strong paper or very thin cardboard. A good size to start with is 10 x 15cm (6 x 4in). Label the corners red and blue as shown.

With the wrong side up, fold up one of the blue corners as if to make a square. Then unfold it.

Make sure the middle pops up.

Fold the other blue corner in the same way. Then unfold it. Mark the ends of the new creases yellow on both sides.

Smaller frogs jump higher.

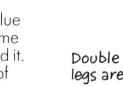

Double legs are more springy.

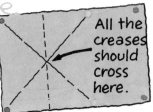

All the creases should cross here.

Turn the paper over. Fold the blue corners to the yellow marks. Then unfold them.

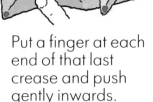

Put a finger at each end of that last crease and push gently inwards.

If your creases are firmly made, the middle will pop up, bringing the blue corners towards the yellow marks.

Make a high jump

Use coins and a thin strip of cardboard for the bar.

Add two more coins each time your frog clears the bar.

Here are some tips to make your frog jump higher:

Bend the front and back legs back a second time.

Or use springy cardboard, like a birthday card.

Or make a tiny frog. Smaller ones jump higher.

Bend the front legs like this

Bend the back legs like this.

Colour your frog with spots.

Flatten the blue corners beneath the yellow marks and turn the paper over.

Point

Fold the blue corners up to the point. This makes the front feet.

Find this edge.

Find the edges between the red and yellow marks. Fold them in to meet in the middle.

Add stripes.

Fold the side with the red dots over the front feet so that just the point sticks out.

Then fold the edge with the red dots back again to meet the last fold.

Turn your frog over. Pull the front feet down a little to make it stand straight.

Draw on eyes.

To make the frog jump, press down in the middle of its back at the edge of the paper. Let your finger slide off.

Target jumping

Make a lily pond target and practise jumping your frog into the middle of it.

Cut a large blue paper circle for a pond.

Draw on lots of lilies and write different scores on each one. See who has most points after three jumps.

49

Bombs away

1. Use a square of strong paper. With the coloured side up, fold it in half from side to side. Then unfold it.

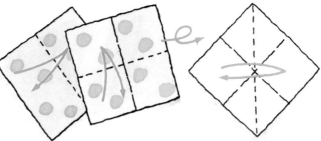

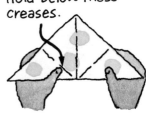

Hold below these creases.

2. Fold it in half from bottom to top. Unfold it and then turn the paper over.

3. Turn one corner towards you. Fold the side corners together and then unfold them.

4. Fold the bottom corner to the top corner. Pick up the paper and hold it at the bottom edge.

Leave this corner on the table.

Point

New Corner

Pocket

5. Push gently inwards. The top corners will move out and the side ones will move in.

6. Fold the front corner to one side and the back corner to the other side.

7. Press the paper flat on a table. Then fold the top two corners to the bottom point.

8. Fold the new corners into the middle. Look for the pockets this makes. You will need them later.

Push here to make the pocket open.

TRICKY

Point

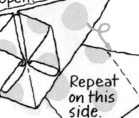

Repeat on this side.

Blow here.

9. Find the two corners at the bottom point. Fold them to the edge of the pockets. Fold them across the pockets. Unfold the last fold only and tuck the corners inside the pockets.

10. Turn the paper over and repeat from step 7.

11. Blow into the small hole at the bottom of the bomb to puff it up.

To charge the bomb pour some water into the hole. Throw it at a target, but only do it outdoors.

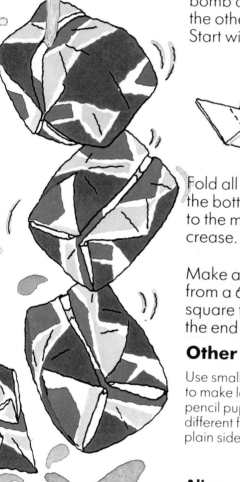

When it lands it will burst and soak whatever it hits.

⭐⭐⭐ White rabbit

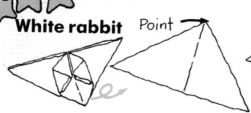

Point

Make an L-shape like this.

Bottom tips

Fold in the same way as the water bomb as far as step 9. Then use the other side to make the ears. Start with the point at the top.

Fold the side edges in to meet the middle crease.

Fold the bottom tips out to the side.

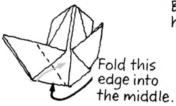

Fold this edge into the middle.

Blow here.

Add eyes and whiskers.

Paint its ears and nose pink.

Fold all the layers at the bottom edge up to the middle crease.

Lift the ears up and hold them together. Pull down the bottom flaps.

Blow through the hole to inflate the rabbit's head.

Make a small rabbit from a 6cm (2½in) square to stick on the end of a pencil.

Tip

If the head wobbles glue it to the end of the pencil.

Robot

Use silver paper for the head (not kitchen foil because it tears).

Stick on a nose, eyes and mouth.

Use large pins for antennae.

Other ideas

Use small waterbombs to make lots of different pencil puppets. Paint a different face on each plain side.

Alien

Pull out the corners from the top pockets to make ears.

Ghost

Use felt tips to draw a face.

Drape a thin white hanky over the pencil. Then stick the head on top.

Finger puppets

Wizard

Use paper which has one white side. You need a 9cm (3in) square for the body and a 6cm (2in) square for the head.

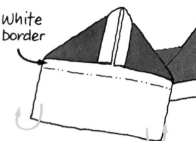

White border

To make the body

Take the big square, white side up. Fold the sides together and unfold them.

Turn the paper over. Fold down ½cm (¼in) at the top.

Turn the paper over again and fold the top corners into the centre.

Fold the bottom edge behind, leaving a white border beneath the coloured triangles.

Turn it around and stand it up to see the finished body.

To make the head

Use the small square. Have one corner towards you, white side up.

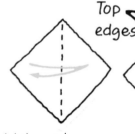

Fold the side corners together. Then unfold them.

Top edges

Make the corners meet here.

Fold the two edges at the top into the middle crease.

Fold here.

Fold the same corner back again from ½cm (¼in) above the last fold.

Leave a small triangle for the face.

Hat

Beard

Fold down the top of the hat and add a sticky gold star on the end of it.

Turn the paper over. Fold in the sides. Make them cross in the middle.

Tuck the right side into the left side. Push it in as far as the fold.

Fold here.

Turn the paper over to press the fold flat. Then fold the sides in.

Hole for your finger.

Tuck the right side into the left side. Push it as far as the fold. This leaves a hole in the middle.

Find the corners in the middle. Fold them both out to meet the side edges.

This is the widest bit.

Now fold the bottom corner up along the widest bit of the paper.

Other ideas

Use different coloured paper to make new puppets. Try changing the hat and cloak.

Green elf

Curl the hat forwards round a pencil. Roll the cloak back.

Wise old man

Stick the head on upside down for a very long beard.

Santa Claus

Use Christmas wrapping paper. Tuck small gifts and rolled up paper into the top of his sack.

Santa Claus

Green elf

Wise old man

Add cotton wool to his head and beard.

Sleepy head

Sleepy head

You could use just the head. Make it from a 9cm (3in) square. Use striped paper for the nightcap. Add cotton wool for a pom pom.

Draw on a face.

Add glue to secure the head.

Balance the head on the body.

Stick star and moon shapes on the hat and cloak.

Then put it on your finger.

53

Jewellery

All the things on the next pages are made from the same base. The blue box in the middle of this page shows how to make it.

To make half a bead

You need two halves to make a whole bead. First make a preliminary base as shown in the blue box. Then continue like this:

Tip

Press down at the bottom of the fold first and smooth upwards, making sure the middle creases meet.

Open ends

Match these creases.

1. Turn the left flap so that it sticks up in the air. Then squash fold it flat, starting at the bottom.

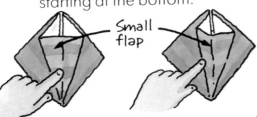

Small flap

2. Turn the paper over and repeat step 1.

3. Fold the small flap on the left over to the right.

Big flap

Small flap

4. Make the big flap on the left stand up and then squash fold it flat as before.

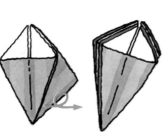

5. Turn the paper over and repeat steps 3 and 4. When you finish, there should be four flaps on each side.

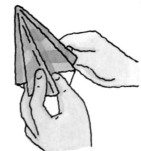

6. Fan out the flaps in a circle to complete the half bead.

To make a preliminary base

Take one square, coloured side up. Make two creases by folding the opposite corners together.

Leave the paper folded in half from bottom to top and hold it along the fold, as shown.

Fold the flap in front to the right and the flap behind to the left.

Make the centre folds meet.

Turn the paper over. Make two more creases by folding the paper in half from side to side and from bottom to top.

Gently bring your fingers together so that all the corners meet in the middle.

Flatten the paper to finish the base. Check there are two flaps on each side.

Slotting two halves together

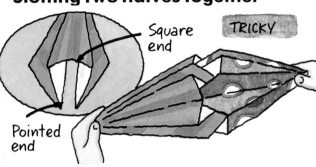

TRICKY

Square end

Pointed end

When you have made two halves, join them like this: slot the pointed ends of each half under the square ends of the other.

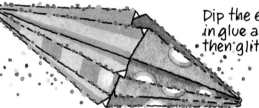

Dip the edges in glue and then glitter.

Make a large bead first, it's easier. Then see how small you can make your beads. Use them to make necklaces or earrings.

Add small waterbombs as round beads (see page 50).

Make a loop to go around your ear.

Tip

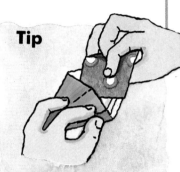

First fit the two halves together roughly. Then work your way around the bead, slotting one point in at a time.

To thread the beads

Use thin wire, such as fuse wire, to make a long needle. Make a loop at one end and tie on some thread.

Make sure your needle is longer than the bead.

Snip off each end of the bead to make a hole to thread through.

Remember to tie a knot at the end of the thread.

Flapping bird

The bird base is used as a starting point for many origami models. The flapping bird is one of them. Another famous one is the crane which is a symbol of good luck in Japan.

To make the bird base

1. Start with a preliminary base from page 54. Turn it so that the open ends are towards you.

Leave this flap on the table.

2. Fold the bottom edges of the top flaps only into the middle. Crease well. Then unfold them.

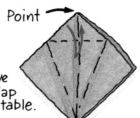

Point

3. Make a strong crease across the top by folding down the point. Then unfold it.

TRICKY

4. Lift up the top flap only at the corner nearest you. Put a finger on the others to keep them on the table.

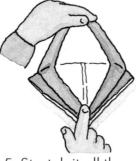

5. Stretch it all the way over the point, bending at the crease you made in step 3. The sides

should fold inwards along the creases you made in step 2. Press it down flat.

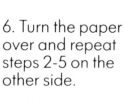

6. Turn the paper over and repeat steps 2-5 on the other side.

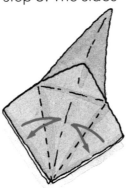

This is the finished bird base.

56

Hang more straws and birds from the other end.

Tip

Check that your mobile balances each time you add a new straw.

If one side is too heavy move the thread in the middle towards the heavy side.

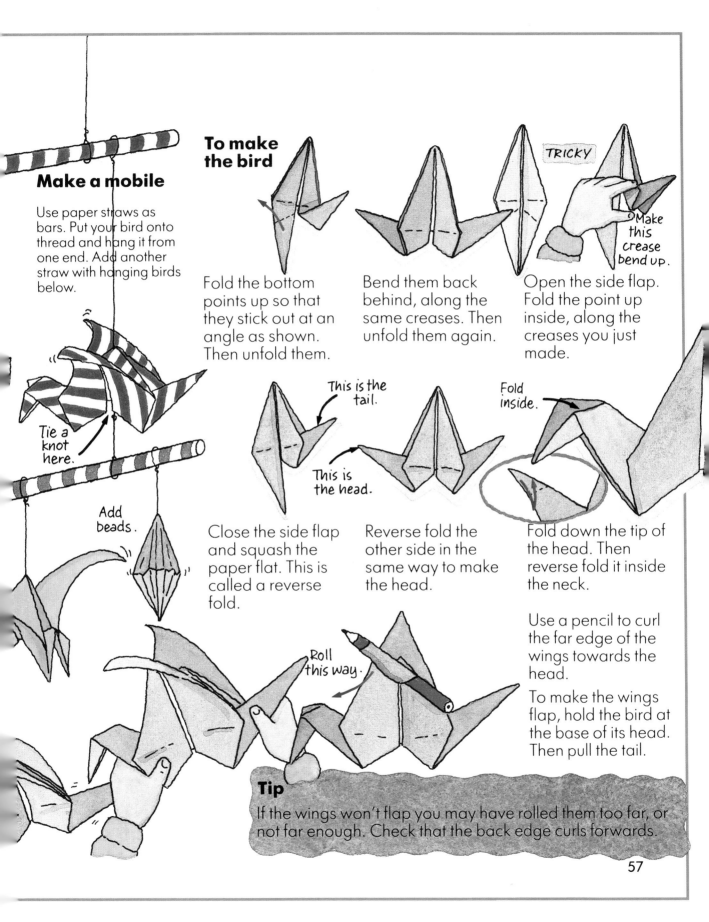

Make a mobile

Use paper straws as bars. Put your bird onto thread and hang it from one end. Add another straw with hanging birds below.

Tie a knot here.

Add beads.

To make the bird

Fold the bottom points up so that they stick out at an angle as shown. Then unfold them.

Bend them back behind, along the same creases. Then unfold them again.

TRICKY

Make this crease bend up.

Open the side flap. Fold the point up inside, along the creases you just made.

This is the tail.

This is the head.

Fold inside.

Close the side flap and squash the paper flat. This is called a reverse fold.

Reverse fold the other side in the same way to make the head.

Fold down the tip of the head. Then reverse fold it inside the neck.

Use a pencil to curl the far edge of the wings towards the head.

To make the wings flap, hold the bird at the base of its head. Then pull the tail.

Roll this way.

Tip

If the wings won't flap you may have rolled them too far, or not far enough. Check that the back edge curls forwards.

57

Star box

This box is also made from a preliminary base. You could use it as a jewellery box. Use wrapping paper or decorate your own paper before you start, as shown below.

To decorate the paper

Stick two sheets of wrapping paper together (see gift boxes on page 37). You could use gold paper for a really striking rim.

Or use plain coloured paper and paint a pattern on one side, starting in the middle.

1. Start by making a preliminary base (see page 54). Turn the paper so that the open ends are towards you.

Open ends

2. Fold the bottom edges of the top flaps only into the middle crease.

Bottom edges

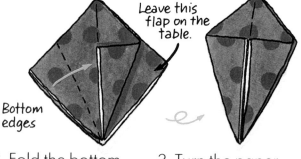

Leave this flap on the table.

3. Turn the paper over and repeat step 2.

6. Turn the paper over and repeat steps 4 and 5.

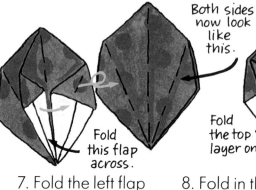

Fold this flap across.

7. Fold the left flap over to the right. Turn the paper over and do the same on the other side.

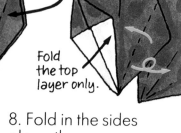

Both sides now look like this.

Fold the top layer only.

8. Fold in the sides along the creases already there. Then turn the paper over.

Leave these bits on the table.

Make the fold for step 12 here.

11. Fold the top flap only up to the cross where the two creases meet.

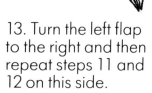

Hold here as you fold.

12. Fold up again, where the white side meets the coloured side.

13. Turn the left flap to the right and then repeat steps 11 and 12 on this side.

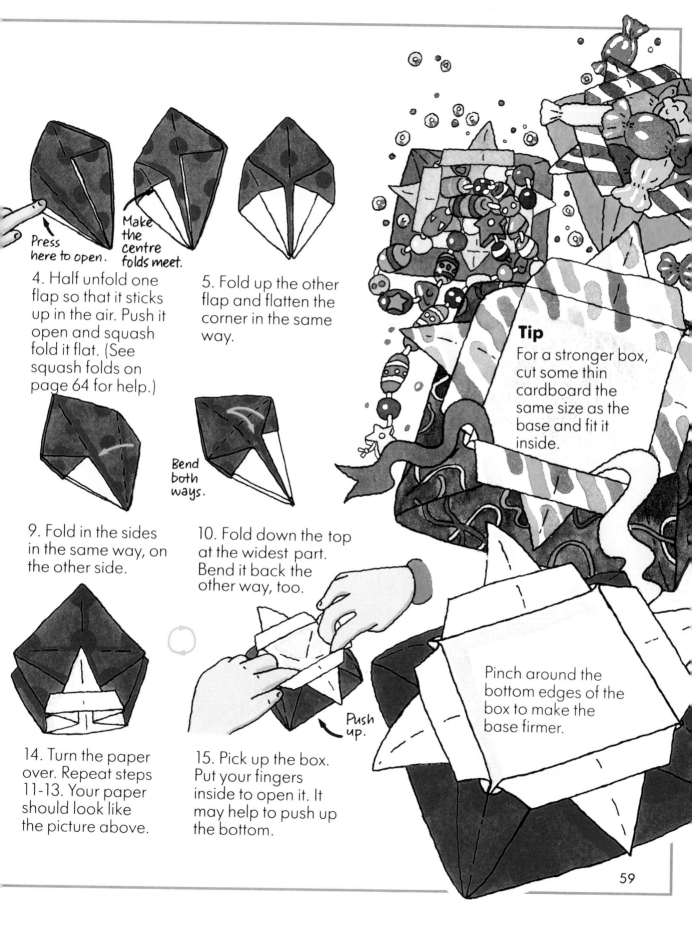

Press here to open.

Make the centre folds meet.

4. Half unfold one flap so that it sticks up in the air. Push it open and squash fold it flat. (See squash folds on page 64 for help.)

5. Fold up the other flap and flatten the corner in the same way.

Bend both ways.

9. Fold in the sides in the same way, on the other side.

10. Fold down the top at the widest part. Bend it back the other way, too.

Push up.

14. Turn the paper over. Repeat steps 11-13. Your paper should look like the picture above.

15. Pick up the box. Put your fingers inside to open it. It may help to push up the bottom.

Tip
For a stronger box, cut some thin cardboard the same size as the base and fit it inside.

Pinch around the bottom edges of the box to make the base firmer.

59

Lily

This is the most difficult model in the book but you can make it using folds you have learned earlier. Use a square of two-coloured paper for the best effect. First fold it into a half bead (see page 54) then continue like this:

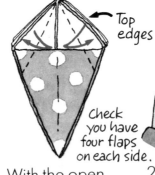

Top edges

Check you have four flaps on each side.

1. With the open ends to the top, fold the top edges of the top flap only into the centre. Then unfold them.

Lift here.

2. Hold the paper down firmly at the top and bottom as shown. Then lift up the top flap.

3. Pull the flap towards you, folding the sides into the middle. They will bend along the creases you made in step 1.

Check all the small triangles are pointing up.

Do the same on the other side too.

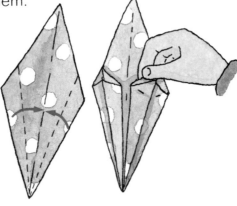

When you have finished your paper should look like this.

7. Turn the left flap over to the right. Then turn the paper over and do the same on the other side.

8. Fold the bottom sides into the middle as shown.

9. Repeat step 8 on the other three sides.

10. Use a pencil to curl each petal. Start on the top flap and then do the same on the three other sides.

Tip

Roll the first petal on the table. Turn the paper over and rest it gently on the table as you roll the second. You will need to open the flower slightly to find the two side petals.

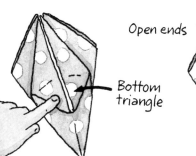

Open ends

Bottom triangle

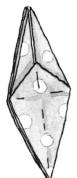

When you have finished your paper should look like this.

4. Squash the bottom triangle down flat. This is the petal fold (see page 64 for help).

5. Fold the bottom triangle up towards the open ends.

6. Now repeat steps 1-5 on the three other sides. See how to do this on the right.

How to repeat a step on three sides

Turn the paper over and repeat for the first time.

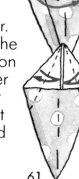

Turn the large flap on the left over to the right and repeat for the second time.

Large flap

Turn the paper over. Then turn the large flap on the left over to the right and repeat for the third time.

Large flap

Bunch of flowers

Use fat, bendy drinking straws for stems.

Tie lots of flowers in a bunch.

Poke the end of the flower in to the straw.

Another idea
Tulip

Take a two-coloured square of paper. Fold all the corners into the middle to make a smaller square.

Use this square, folded side up, to make a waterbomb (see page 50). When you blow it up you will have two-coloured petals.

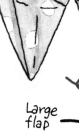

61

Stacking tree

To make the branches

Cut a large green square first. Now cut four more, making each one smaller than the one before.

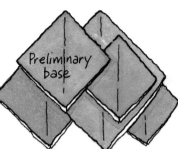

Fold all the squares into preliminary bases (see page 54). Then continue like this for each one.

1. With the open end of the base towards you, fold up the top flap. Then unfold it.

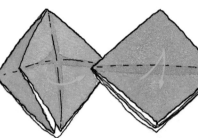

2. Do the same on the other three sides (see the tip on page 61 for help).

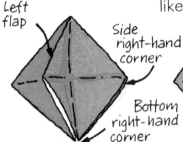

Left flap

Side right-hand corner

Bottom right-hand corner

3. Turn the left flap so that it sticks up in the air.

Small triangle

4. Take the bottom right-hand corner up to meet the side right-hand corner.

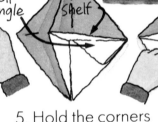

Shelf

TRICKY

5. Hold the corners firmly together. Then flatten the small triangle below to make a little shelf.

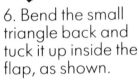

6. Bend the small triangle back and tuck it up inside the flap, as shown.

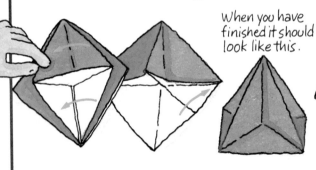

When you have finished it should look like this.

7. Lift the right flap up so the shelf goes over to the left. Then repeat steps 4-6 on the next flap.

8. Fold the two flaps on the other side in the same way. You will need to pick the paper up.

Tip

The last little triangle may be tricky to fold inside. Try opening up the paper a little and pushing it in with a finger.

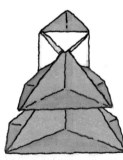

9. When all the branches are folded, slot one on top of the other.

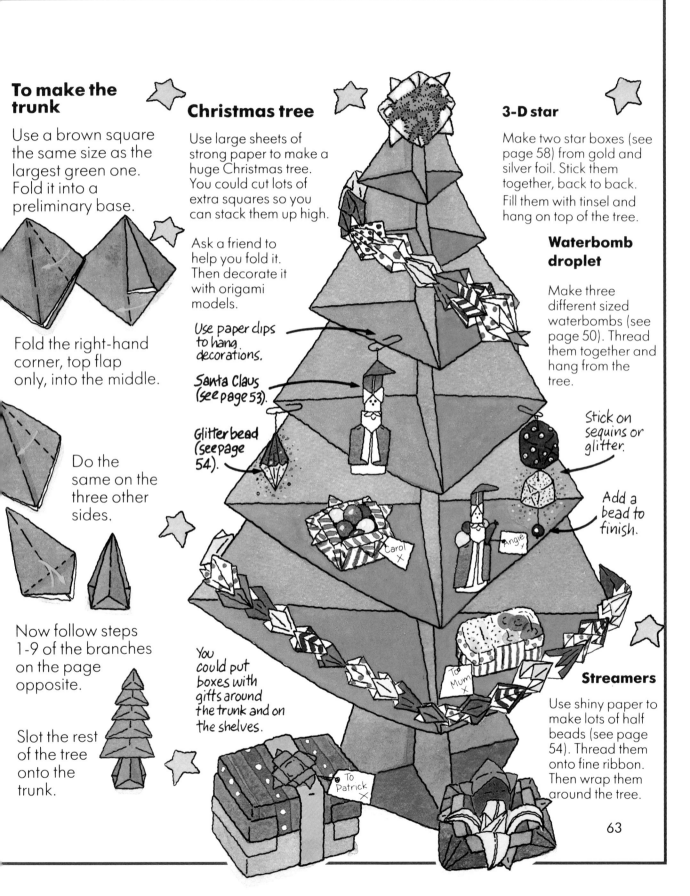

To make the trunk

Use a brown square the same size as the largest green one. Fold it into a preliminary base.

Fold the right-hand corner, top flap only, into the middle.

Do the same on the three other sides.

Now follow steps 1-9 of the branches on the page opposite.

Slot the rest of the tree onto the trunk.

Christmas tree

Use large sheets of strong paper to make a huge Christmas tree. You could cut lots of extra squares so you can stack them up high.

Ask a friend to help you fold it. Then decorate it with origami models.

Use paper clips to hang decorations.

Santa Claus (see page 53).

Glitter bead (see page 54).

You could put boxes with gifts around the trunk and on the shelves.

3-D star

Make two star boxes (see page 58) from gold and silver foil. Stick them together, back to back. Fill them with tinsel and hang on top of the tree.

Waterbomb droplet

Make three different sized waterbombs (see page 50). Thread them together and hang from the tree.

Stick on sequins or glitter.

Add a bead to finish.

Streamers

Use shiny paper to make lots of half beads (see page 54). Thread them onto fine ribbon. Then wrap them around the tree.

Tricky folds

Some folds are used over and over again in lots of different origami models, so it is useful to remember how to do them. Here are three tricky folds which you have learned in this book and may find useful for other models.

The origami models in this book that are not traditional were designed by Sarah Goodall (Fearsome fangs); Nick Robinson (Crown); Susanna Kricskovics (Finger puppets); Makoto Yamaguchi (Stacking tree and tulip).

If you would like to find out more about origami and learn how to make more models, you could contact Dave Brill at the British Origami Society, 253 Park Lane, Poynton, Stockport SK12 1RH.

Reverse fold

First make a strong crease where shown by bending the paper both ways.

Then open the paper out above the crease you just made.

Finally, push the paper above the crease down, so that it folds inside the rest of the paper.

Squash fold

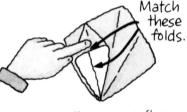

First lift up the corner that is going to be squashed flat.

Then open the corner by pressing along the fold.

Finally press it flat, starting at the bottom. Keep the two centre folds together.

Petal fold

First make all the preparation creases. Press down firmly to make them really strong.

Then lift up the edge of the top layer. Hold the other layers firmly on the table.

Finally, stretch the edge of the top layer down towards you. The paper will fold along the creases you made earlier.

PAPER SUPERPLANES

Contents

66 Getting started

68 Square-o-plane

70 Delta wing

72 Flying squirrel

74 Tiny trainers
(V jet, A10 Warthog)

76 Camber jet

78 Stunt bug

80 Seagull

82 Concorde

84 Sky rocket

86 Swing wing

88 Superglider

93 Templates

Getting started

This part of the book shows you how to make lots of amazing paper planes and tells you how to fly them. It starts with small models, marked ☆, that you make up quickly from a single piece of paper. The ones marked ☆☆☆ are much bigger and take a couple of hours to put together carefully. These two pages tell you all the things you need to know before you start.

What sort of paper?

It is very important to have the right type of paper for each model. If it is too floppy or too heavy the plane will not fly well. This book talks about the three different thicknesses of paper shown below:

How to score a line

Scoring a line is when you make a firm crease in the paper. Score lines are used to fold along, or to strengthen a wing. You make one like this:

Put a ruler along the line you want to score. Hold it there firmly.

Use a ball point pen to draw a line against the ruler. Press hard to make a firm crease.

Things you will need

Scissors

Pencil

Thin cardboard such as the sort used for cereal packets.

Strong white glue, such as PVA or UHU.

Stick of glue

Plasticine*

Stiff paper, about the thickness of the pages in this book, such as top quality writing paper or envelopes.

An old ball-point pen to score with – if it has run out of ink it won't mark your plane.

Ruler

Normal paper, such as ordinary writing paper or photocopy paper.

Sticky tape-masking tape is best because it peels off easily.

Metal paper-clips

Tracing paper

*U.S. Plastic modelling compound.

Folding

When you make a paper plane it is very important to fold accurately and neatly.

Press down in the middle first. Then smooth out to the sides.

For long folds, place the line you want to fold along on the edge of a table. Then press down against it.

Decoration

Only use decorations that won't change the shape or weight of your plane. You could start with coloured paper or use felt tip pens to draw on patterns afterwards.

Wet paints make the paper wrinkle. Enamel paints are too heavy.

Spray paints shrink the paper and make it curl.

Launching a plane

These angles must be the same.

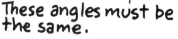

Before you launch a plane, always check to see that both sides look exactly the same and that the wings tilt up at the same angle on each side.

Light models with big wings, like squirrel and superglider, fly slowly so you need to launch them gently. Move your whole arm slowly forwards and then let go.

Heavier models with smaller wings, like stunt bug and sky rocket, fly faster and need harder launches. Throw them very slightly upwards.

Square-o-plane

This simple design shows you what makes a paper plane fly. Use a normal piece of paper, such as ordinary writing paper, 21 x 15cm (6 x 8in).

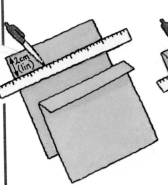

Make the last score line here.

Middle

Use felt tip pens to draw on a face or bright pattern.

1. Score a line 2cm (1in) from the top of one short edge (see 'How to score' on page 66). Then fold along it.

2. Score another line at the edge of the last fold and fold over again. Then repeat this once more.

3. Turn the paper over so that the folded edge is underneath. Mark the middle of each short edge.

Use a large metal paper-clip. Put it in the middle.

Bend down

Bend up

Long edges

short edges

4. Score a line down the centre. Fold along it, then unfold it, so that the sides tilt up slightly.

5. Make a pencil dot on the long edges, 2cm (1in) from each corner as shown.

6. Score a line from each pencil dot to the centre of the short edge.

7. Bend the front corners down slightly and the back corners up. Add a paper-clip to the front edge.

Before you launch your plane, check that it looks like the pictures below from the side and the front.

Side view

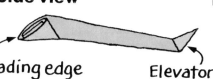

Leading edge   Elevator

The front edge needs to be heavier. It is called the leading edge. The back corners tilt up and are called elevators. They help stop the plane from rocking.

Front view

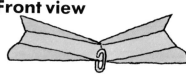

The wings tilt slightly up at exactly the same angle. This is called dihedral. It makes the plane glide steadily.

To launch the square-o-plane

Hold the plane at the back with one finger on top. Launch with a gentle push. Don't throw it, just let go. If it doesn't make a perfect glide, try changing the balance as described below.

Bend the corners up more.

Add a paper-clip.

A stall is when the tail drops down because the nose is not heavy enough. Add another paper-clip or flatten out the elevators.

A dive is when the nose drops down because it is too heavy. Bend the back corners up, or take away a paper-clip.

Perfect glide

Stall

A slight stall may mean you launched it too fast.

Dive

A slight dive may mean you launched it too slowly.

69

Delta wing

You need a piece of normal paper 20cm x 28cm (8in x 11in). Have the short edges of the paper at the sides.

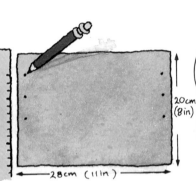

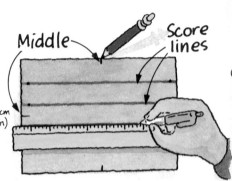

Tip

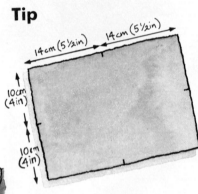

To find the middle of the side edges, measure 10cm (4in) from each corner. For the long edges measure 14cm (5½in).

1. Make a pencil dot 4cm, 8cm and 12cm (1½in, 3in and 4½in) below the top edge, on both sides.

2. Score a line between each pair of dots. Then mark the middle of each edge.

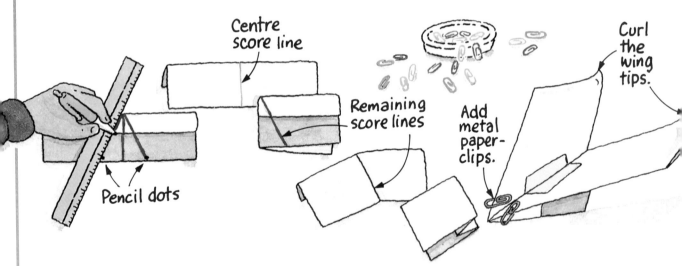

7. Score a line from each dot to the centre of the folded edge.

8. Turn the paper over. Then fold it down the centre score line.

9. Fold the wings back along the remaining score lines.

10. Make the wings stick out to the side. Tape down the middle and add paper-clips.

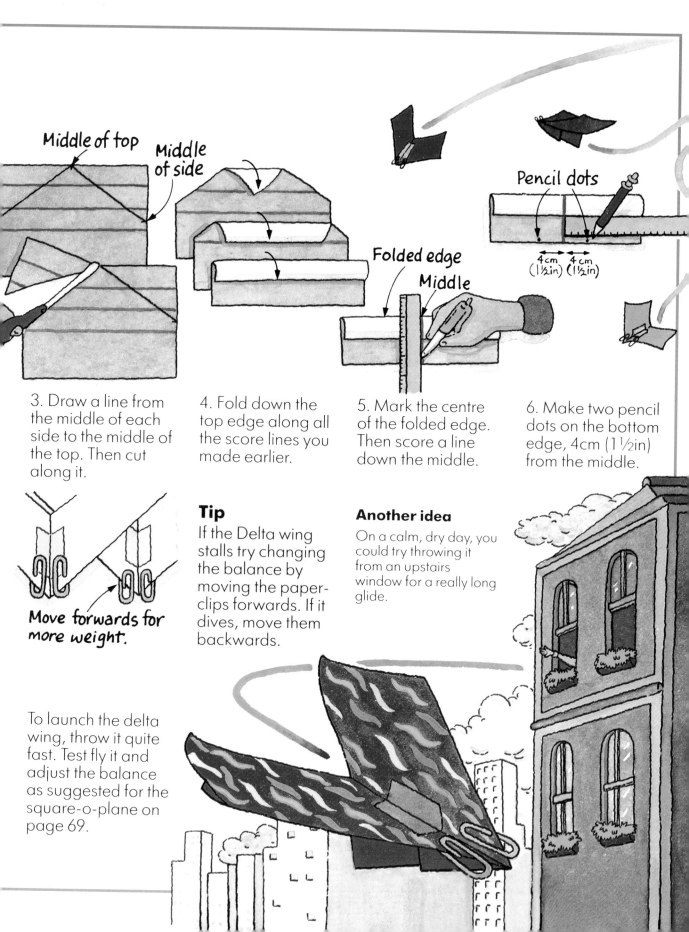

Middle of top **Middle of side**

Pencil dots

4cm 4cm
(1½in) (1½in)

Folded edge
Middle

3. Draw a line from the middle of each side to the middle of the top. Then cut along it.

4. Fold down the top edge along all the score lines you made earlier.

5. Mark the centre of the folded edge. Then score a line down the middle.

6. Make two pencil dots on the bottom edge, 4cm (1½in) from the middle.

Move forwards for more weight.

Tip
If the Delta wing stalls try changing the balance by moving the paperclips forwards. If it dives, move them backwards.

Another idea
On a calm, dry day, you could try throwing it from an upstairs window for a really long glide.

To launch the delta wing, throw it quite fast. Test fly it and adjust the balance as suggested for the square-o-plane on page 69.

Flying squirrel

Lots of models in this part of the book use templates. It tells you how to copy a template on page 93. For the squirrel you need the green one on page 94.

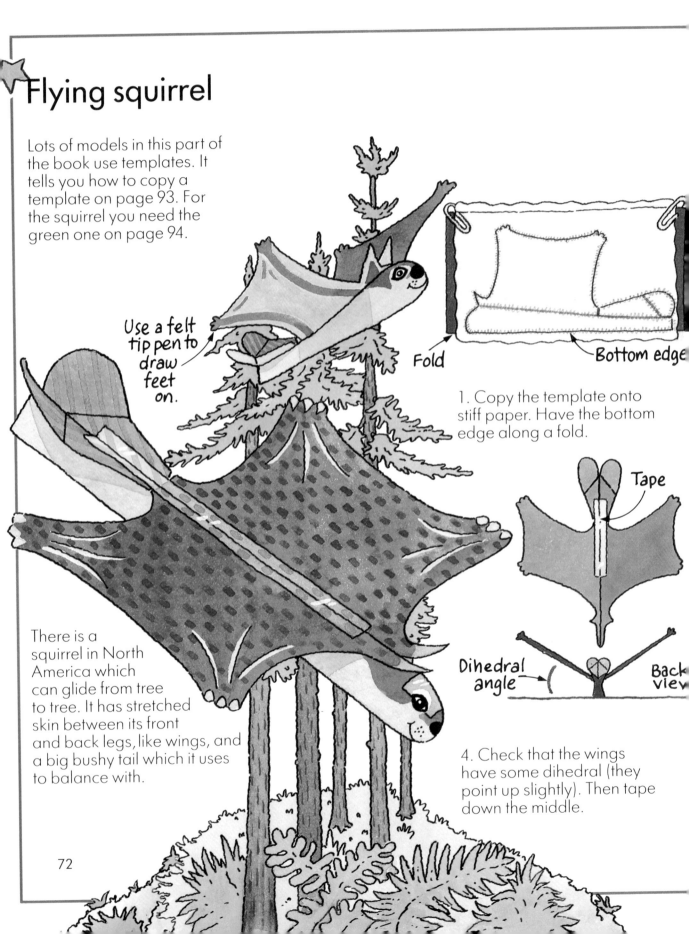

Use a felt tip pen to draw feet on.

Fold

Bottom edge

1. Copy the template onto stiff paper. Have the bottom edge along a fold.

Tape

Dihedral angle

Back view

There is a squirrel in North America which can glide from tree to tree. It has stretched skin between its front and back legs, like wings, and a big bushy tail which it uses to balance with.

4. Check that the wings have some dihedral (they point up slightly). Then tape down the middle.

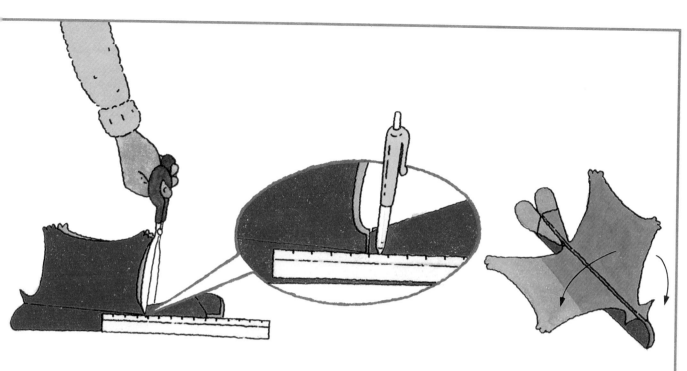

2. Cut along the red lines
and score the blue ones.
The blue line changes angle
at the slit, so you will need
to score each side
separately.

3. Bend the wings and tail
out to the side along the
score lines.

Tip

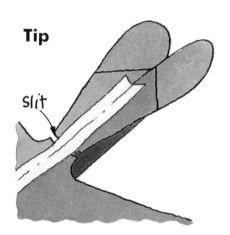

Slit

If you put the tape on
carefully, it will hold the
wings and tail at the right
dihedral angle. It will also
keep the tail pointing up
slightly at the slit.

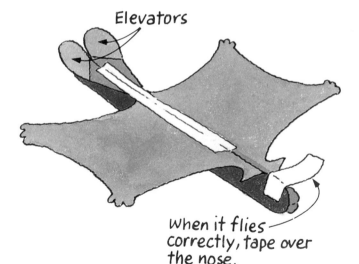

Elevators

when it flies
correctly, tape over
the nose.

5. Bend the ends of the tail
up slightly along the
remaining score lines to
make elevators.

6. Put plasticine inside the
nose to add weight. Then
test fly it. If it dives, bend the
elevators up more. If it stalls,
take some plasticine away.

Tiny trainers

These two tiny planes are made from a single piece of paper and are quick to put together. Use normal paper, such as ordinary writing paper or photocopy paper for both of them.

V jet

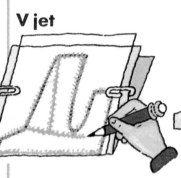

Cut here

1. Copy the pink template on page 93, onto a piece of folded paper. Place the bottom edge of the template on the fold.

2. Score along the blue lines and cut along the red slit. The bottom blue line changes angle at the slit, so score each side separately.

3. Bend the wings and tail out to the sides along the score lines. The wings should point up slightly. The tail should make a 'V'.

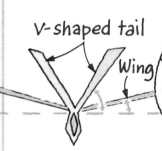

V-shaped tail

Wing

Tape holds the wings and tail at the right angle.

Add plasticine

4. Check that your plane looks like the picture above, from behind. Then use tape to hold the wings and tail at the correct angles.

5. Put plasticine inside the nose. Then test fly the plane. If it stalls, add more plasticine; if it dives, take some away.

6. When the V jet is properly balanced, you can try steering it with the tail. It tells you how on the right.

Steering V jet

Twist one side of the tail up and the other side down to make the V jet turn.

Curl the tip of the tail between your finger and thumb like this:

Tail

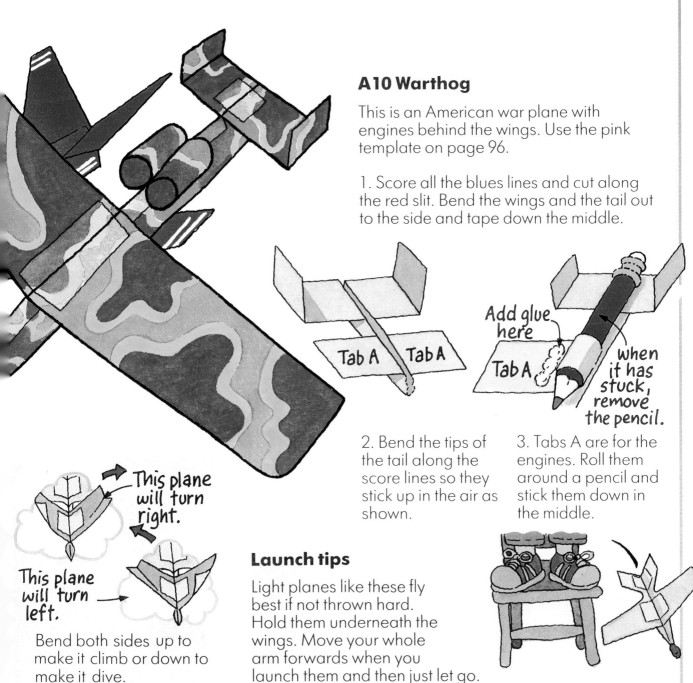

A10 Warthog

This is an American war plane with engines behind the wings. Use the pink template on page 96.

1. Score all the blues lines and cut along the red slit. Bend the wings and the tail out to the side and tape down the middle.

Tab A   Tab A

Add glue here

Tab A

when it has stuck, remove the pencil.

2. Bend the tips of the tail along the score lines so they stick up in the air as shown.

3. Tabs A are for the engines. Roll them around a pencil and stick them down in the middle.

This plane will turn right.

This plane will turn left.

Bend both sides up to make it climb or down to make it dive.

Launch tips

Light planes like these fly best if not thrown hard. Hold them underneath the wings. Move your whole arm forwards when you launch them and then just let go.

The higher you launch it, the further it will fly. Try standing on a chair and see how far it will glide.

⭐ Camber jet

This plane has a curved wing, called a cambered wing, which makes it fly better. See below if you want to know why.

What makes a wing lift

When the wing goes forward, some air goes over the top of it and some goes below it.

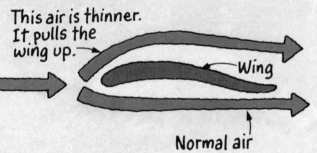

This air is thinner. It pulls the wing up.

Wing

Normal air

If the wing is curved, the air on the top has further to go than the air below. So the top air stretches out to catch up with the bottom air. This makes it thinner, like a vaccuum, and sucks the wing up.

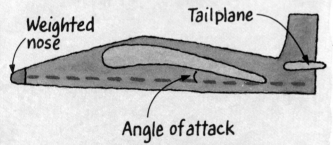

Weighted nose

Tailplane

Angle of attack

The tailplane, or elevators, and the heavy nose balance the wing so that it stays at the angle that will give it the best lift. This is called 'the angle of attack'.

76

1. Copy the purple template on page 94 onto stiff paper. Only trace the solid lines, the dotted ones are for the next model.

2. Cut along the red lines. Score the blues ones very firmly so that it makes a crease on both sides of the fold.

Pre-flight check

Look under the wings of your plane for the dots you traced from the template. These mark the centre of balance. Place the wings on the tips of two pencils, alongside the dots.

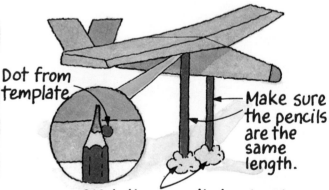

Dot from template

Make sure the pencils are the same length.

Stick the pencils in plasticine.

If the plane falls backwards, add plasticine to the nose. If it falls forwards take some away. When it balances, the wings will be at the right angle of attack.

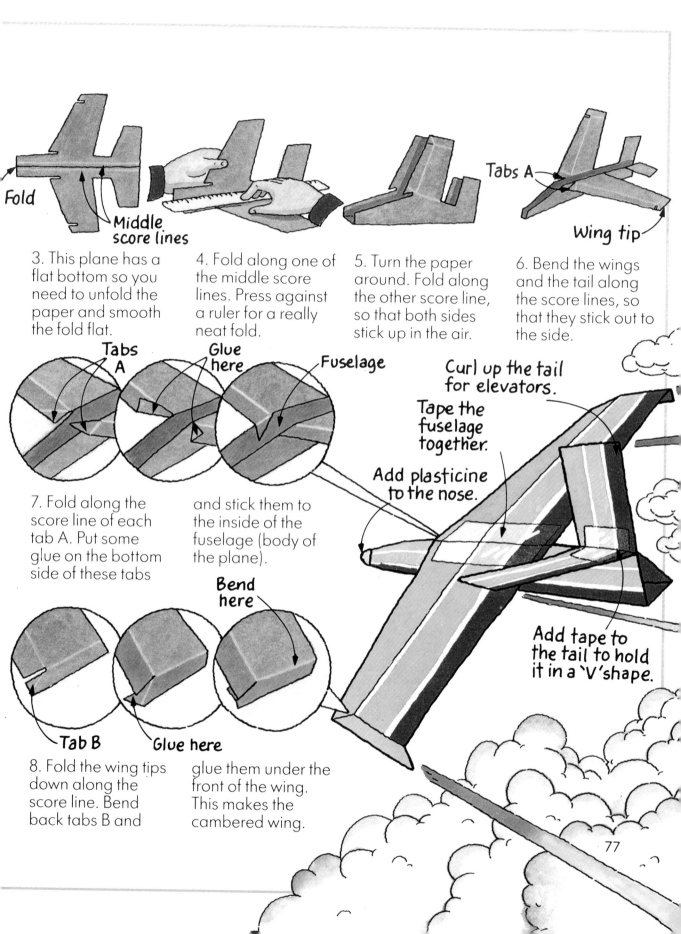

Fold

Middle score lines

Tabs A

Wing tip

3. This plane has a flat bottom so you need to unfold the paper and smooth the fold flat.

4. Fold along one of the middle score lines. Press against a ruler for a really neat fold.

5. Turn the paper around. Fold along the other score line, so that both sides stick up in the air.

6. Bend the wings and the tail along the score lines, so that they stick out to the side.

Tabs A

Glue here

Fuselage

7. Fold along the score line of each tab A. Put some glue on the bottom side of these tabs

and stick them to the inside of the fuselage (body of the plane).

Curl up the tail for elevators.

Tape the fuselage together.

Add plasticine to the nose.

Bend here

Add tape to the tail to hold it in a 'V' shape.

Tab B

Glue here

8. Fold the wing tips down along the score line. Bend back tabs B and

glue them under the front of the wing. This makes the cambered wing.

77

Stunt bug

This plane has extra features which make it fly all sorts of stunts. You need to make it from thin cardboard because it has to fly hard and fast.

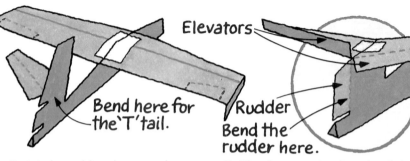

Elevators

Bend here for the 'T' tail.

Rudder

Bend the rudder here.

1. Start by copying the purple template on page 94 which you used for the camber jet, but this time trace, score and cut all the dotted lines too.

2. Make it like the camber jet, except for the tail. Fold that out to the side along the dotted blue score line to make a T-shape.

3. The bits at the back of the tail are for the rudder. Stick them together. The score lines on the top of the 'T' are for the elevators.

Stunts to do

Before you try these stunts make sure your plane is well balanced and can fly in a straight line. Then try bending the elevators, ailerons or rudder as described on the right.

For all of the stunts you need to launch the plane hard and fast and you need lots of space. A big empty room is best, but you could fly it outside on a calm, dry day.

Loop the loop
Have both elevators up. Hold beneath the wings and launch level.

Snap loop
Have both elevators up and both ailerons down. Launch level.

*The Immelman
Have both elevators up and one aileron down. Launch level.

Barrel roll
Have the elevators up and the rudder to one side. Launch with the nose pointing up slightly.

It flies a big loop.

It flies a tight loop then falls to the ground.

It starts a loop, then rolls back around the right way up.

It flies a loop to one side as if it was flying around a barrel.

* This one is named after the German pilot who invented it.

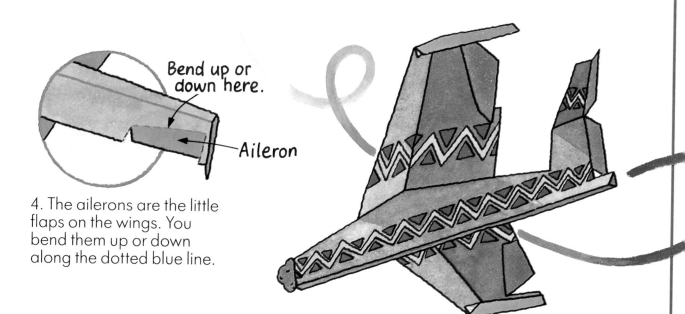

Bend up or down here.

Aileron

4. The ailerons are the little flaps on the wings. You bend them up or down along the dotted blue line.

Slow roll
Have one aileron up, and one down. Launch slightly upwards.

The 'S' bend
Have the rudder to the left. Launch it with the right wing towards the ground.

The 'G' turn
Have the elevators up. Launch with one wing tip pointing straight to the floor.

The outside loop
Have the elevators down; ailerons up. Hold the nose, and launch it straight up.

It flies forwards, rolling sideways as it goes.

It flies to the right and then to the left.

It flies a circle in front of you and comes back to the same place.

It flies a loop with the wings on the outside.

Other ideas
You could set up an obstacle course and see how many launches it takes to get around it. Here are some obstacles you could try.

Fly an 'S' bend around two chairs.

Fly a left or right turn through the door.

Fly a loop around the washing line.

Seagull

You need the orange template on page 95 and stiff paper, folded in half. A large envelope is ideal as long as you keep away from any overlapping edges.

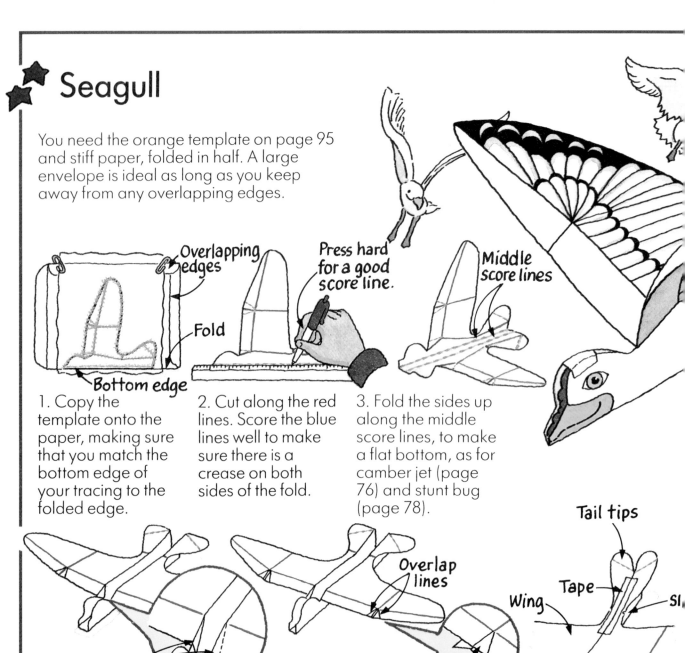

1. Copy the template onto the paper, making sure that you match the bottom edge of your tracing to the folded edge.

2. Cut along the red lines. Score the blue lines well to make sure there is a crease on both sides of the fold.

3. Fold the sides up along the middle score lines, to make a flat bottom, as for camber jet (page 76) and stunt bug (page 78).

4. Bend the wings and tail out to the side. Then glue tabs A inside the body, as you did for the camber jet.

5. Find the two overlap lines either side of the slit, in the middle of the wing. Put some glue on one and slide the other over until the two lines meet. Hold them together until stuck. This gives the wings their bent shape.

6. Bend the tips of the tail up. Tape over the slit where the tail and wings join, to make the tail stick up slightly.

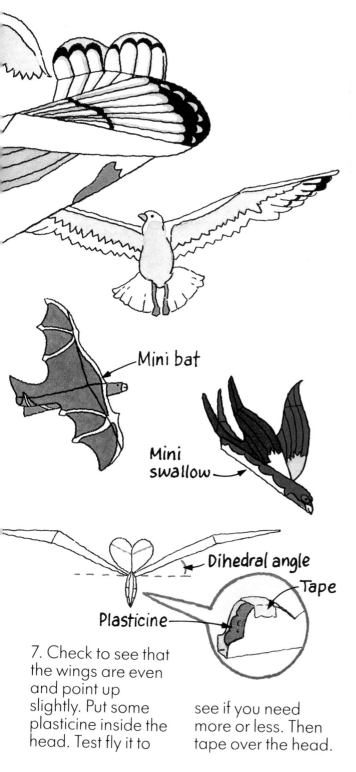

Mini bat

Mini swallow

Dihedral angle

Tape

Plasticine

7. Check to see that the wings are even and point up slightly. Put some plasticine inside the head. Test fly it to see if you need more or less. Then tape over the head.

Other ideas

You could use different shapes for other birds. Try making up the mini templates below.

Small ones are harder to fly so be very neat and careful when you make them. Remember to add plasticine to the head. You could colour in the feathers with felt tip pens.

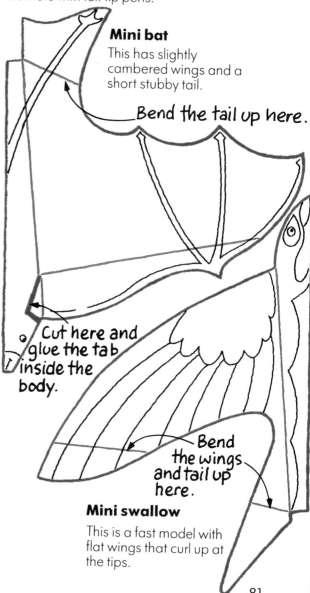

Mini bat
This has slightly cambered wings and a short stubby tail.

Bend the tail up here.

Cut here and glue the tab inside the body.

Bend the wings and tail up here.

Mini swallow
This is a fast model with flat wings that curl up at the tips.

81

Concorde

Concorde is the world's fastest passenger plane. It flies from London to New York in 3 hours, 50 minutes. This model won't go that far but it is pretty fast. You need to glue it very carefully to make the wings the right shape.

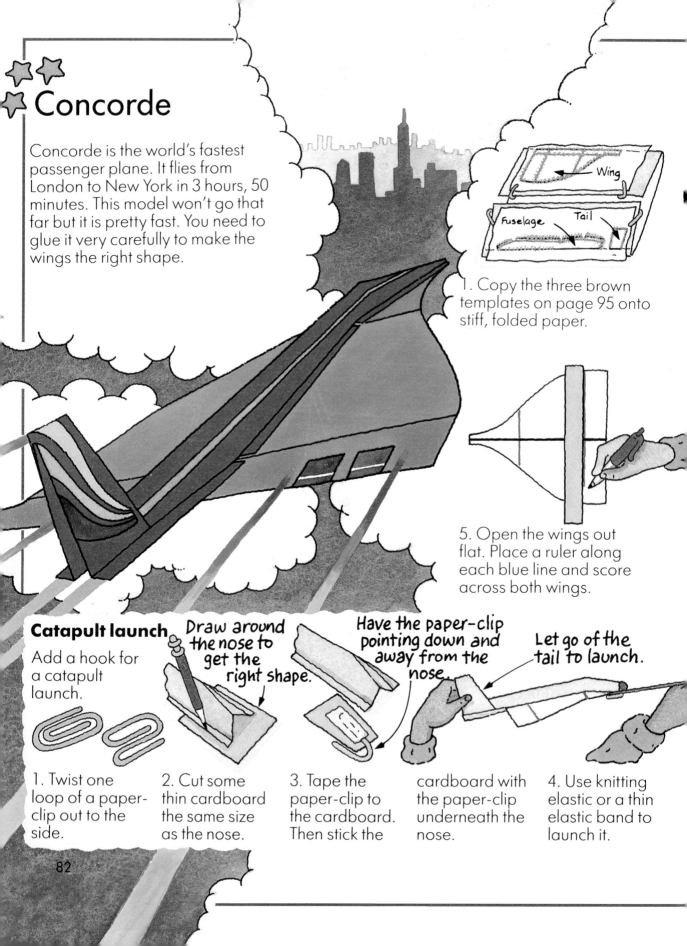

1. Copy the three brown templates on page 95 onto stiff, folded paper.

5. Open the wings out flat. Place a ruler along each blue line and score across both wings.

Catapult launch

Add a hook for a catapult launch.

Draw around the nose to get the right shape.

Have the paper-clip pointing down and away from the nose.

Let go of the tail to launch.

1. Twist one loop of a paper-clip out to the side.

2. Cut some thin cardboard the same size as the nose.

3. Tape the paper-clip to the cardboard. Then stick the cardboard with the paper-clip underneath the nose.

4. Use knitting elastic or a thin elastic band to launch it.

82

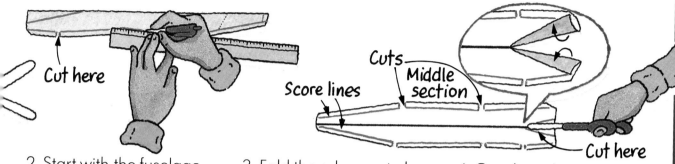

Cut here

Score lines

Cuts

Middle section

Cut here

2. Start with the fuselage. Score each blue line separately. Cut along the red ones.

3. Fold the edges out along the score lines. Do this bit by bit, starting with the section in the middle between the cuts.

4. Cut along the nose end of the fold, to where the blue lines meet the fold. Bend the corners in along the blue lines and glue them inside.

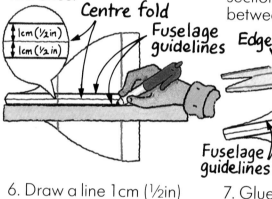

Centre fold

Fuselage guidelines

1cm (½in)
1cm (½in)

Edges

Fuselage guidelines

It bends up at the back.

It bends down at the front.

6. Draw a line 1cm (½in) away from the centre fold, on each side. These are the guidelines for the fuselage.

7. Glue the fuselage to the wings. Make sure that each edge meets the guideline you drew earlier. See the tip

below for help. The shape of the fuselage makes the wings bend down at the nose and up at the tail end.

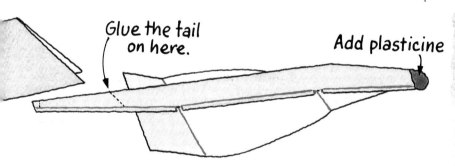

Glue the tail on here.

Add plasticine

8. Finally, take the tail fin. Put glue inside and stick it to the end of the fuselage, behind the wings. Have the

sloping edge towards the nose. Put plasticine in the nose and test fly it.

Tip

To match each edge with the guidelines stick one section at a time, starting in the middle. Hold it together with your thumb and fingers until it has stuck.

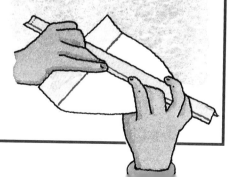

Sky rocket

This is a fast and furious model that you can fly outdoors. Make sure that you fold and glue it neatly, because even a small mistake will change the way it flies.

1. Copy the yellow template on page 95 onto thin cardboard, folded in half. Score all the blue lines carefully.

Use the edge of a table for a straight fold.

Diamond-shaped tube

2. Fold along the long blue lines to make a diamond-shaped tube for the fuselage.

Wings

Tail

Fuselage

3. Fold the wings and the tail out to the sides along the score lines.

Add tape

Hook

4. Bend one side of a paper-clip out to make a hook. Tape around the rest of the paper-clip.

Leave the end of the nose open.

Pinch the edges together until they stick.

Have the hook pointing this way.

Glue the tail fin together too.

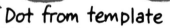
Dot from template

5. Make a hole in the fuselage, at the dot you traced from the template. Push the hook through it.

Make sure it is pointing away from the nose, then stick the taped side of the paper-clip inside.

6. Glue the top of the fuselage and the tail fin together. Leave the nose open for plasticine.

Smooth plasticine around the nose for a soft, safe point.

7. Put the plane upside down on thin cardboard and draw around the edge of the wings. Cut out the shape you have drawn and stick it on top of the wings. Then do exactly the same for the tail.

8. Put plasticine in the nose and test fly the plane. Adjust the amount until it flies well. Then tape around the nose.

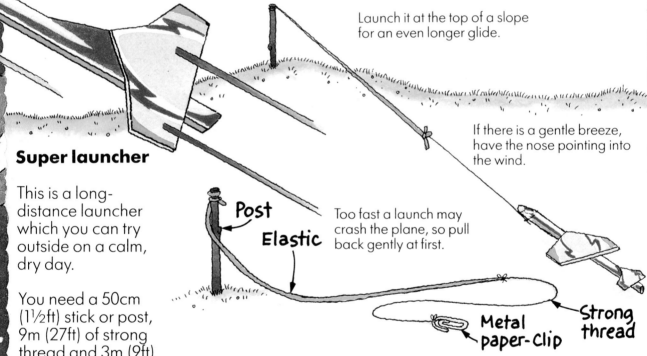

Launch it at the top of a slope for an even longer glide.

If there is a gentle breeze, have the nose pointing into the wind.

Post

Elastic

Too fast a launch may crash the plane, so pull back gently at first.

Metal paper-clip

Strong thread

Super launcher

This is a long-distance launcher which you can try outside on a calm, dry day.

You need a 50cm (1½ft) stick or post, 9m (27ft) of strong thread and 3m (9ft) of 3mm (⅛ in) -wide elastic. You can buy this in model plane shops or ask a sewing shop for thin elastic.

Tie the thread to the elastic, which you then tie to the top of the post. Add a metal paper-clip to the other end of the thread.

Stick the post firmly into the ground and put the paper-clip onto the launch hook of your plane.

Pull the plane away from the post until the elastic is stretched. Point the nose up slightly and let go to launch.

⭐ Swing wing

This model is the same as the sky rocket, only you add wings which move. You need to make the sky rocket on page 84 first. Then add two wings. Follow the steps below for each wing.

To make each wing

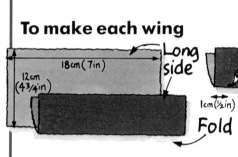

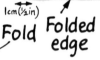

1. Take a piece of stiff paper, 18 x 12cm (7 x 4¾ in). Fold it in half, with the longest sides together.

2. Measure 1cm (½in) from the left corner of the folded edge and from the right corner of the open edge.

3. Draw a line from each measurement to the opposite corner as shown above. Then cut along the lines.

To fix the wings to the sky rocket

Use a pin or cocktail stick to make the hole.

Dots from template

4. Open the paper out. Put some tape over the edge that points outwards.

5. Fold the paper in half again. Cut some tape 12cm (4¾ in) long. Use it to stick the long edges together, starting at the corner without tape.

6. Find the open corner. Measure 1cm (½in) in from each edge. Make a hole where the two measures meet, using a pin or cocktail stick.

1. Make a hole in the rocket wings at the dots you copied from the template.

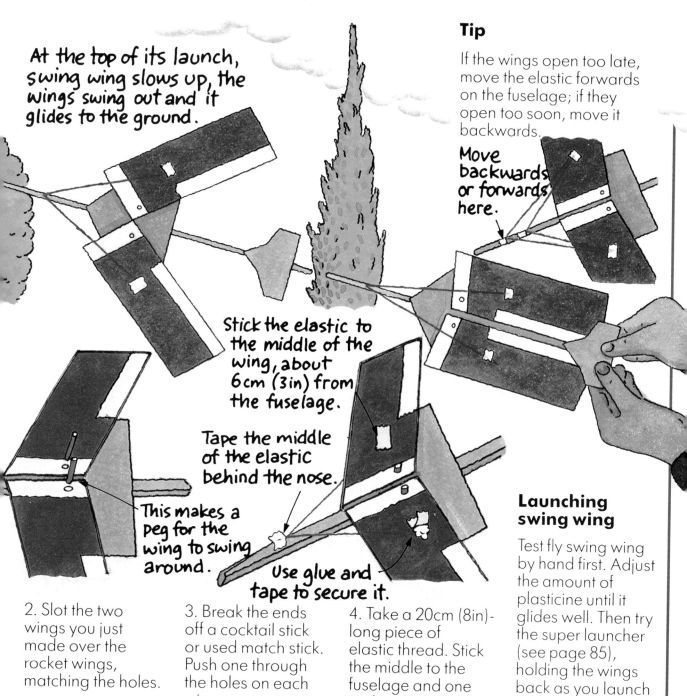

At the top of its launch, swing wing slows up, the wings swing out and it glides to the ground.

Tip

If the wings open too late, move the elastic forwards on the fuselage; if they open too soon, move it backwards.

Move backwards or forwards here.

Stick the elastic to the middle of the wing, about 6cm (3in) from the fuselage.

Tape the middle of the elastic behind the nose.

This makes a peg for the wing to swing around.

Use glue and tape to secure it.

Launching swing wing

Test fly swing wing by hand first. Adjust the amount of plasticine until it glides well. Then try the super launcher (see page 85), holding the wings back as you launch it.

2. Slot the two wings you just made over the rocket wings, matching the holes.

3. Break the ends off a cocktail stick or used match stick. Push one through the holes on each wing.

4. Take a 20cm (8in)-long piece of elastic thread. Stick the middle to the fuselage and one end to each wing.

87

Superglider

This model is quite difficult to make – there are 23 steps to follow – but it is three times bigger than anything else in this book. A well-made model can fly 100m (300ft). Only try making it when you can fold and glue neatly.

You need a large hall to fly it indoors. Or you could try flying it outside on a very calm day when the grass is dry. To start with, you need thin cardboard, thick paper, thin paper, a drinking straw, strong glue and the grey templates on page 96.

To make the wings

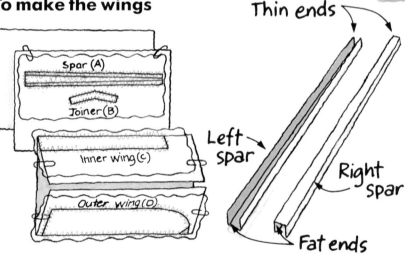

1. Copy templates A and B onto thin cardboard and C and D onto thick paper. Remember to copy each one twice – once for each wing.

2. Score the blue lines of each spar, A, firmly. Fold the edges up along the score lines on one spar, and down the other way on the other, to make a right and left spar.

Use a book to make a neat fold. Place it on one side of the score line. Use a ruler to fold up the other side. Press against the book edge.

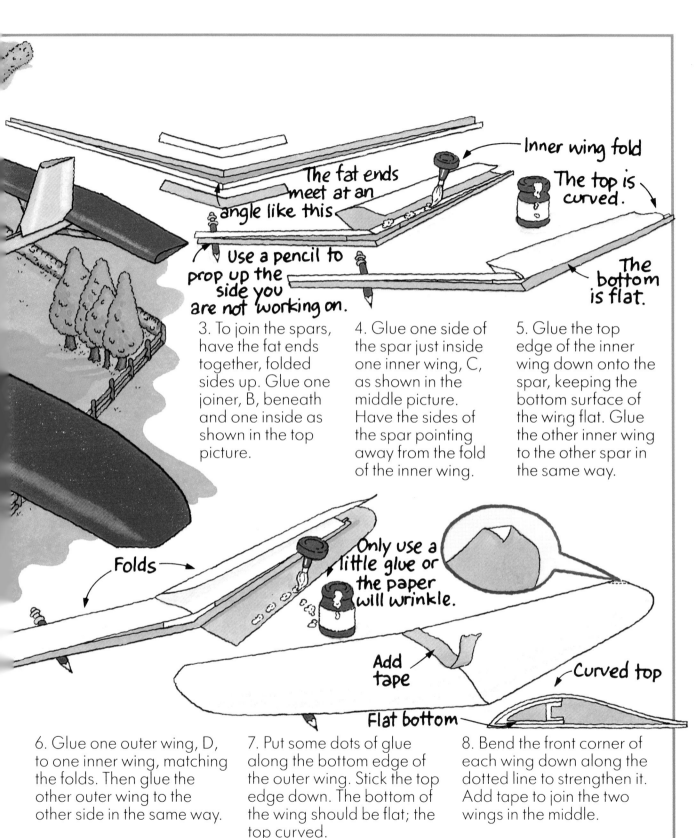

The fat ends meet at an angle like this.

Use a pencil to prop up the side you are not working on.

Inner wing fold

The top is curved.

The bottom is flat.

3. To join the spars, have the fat ends together, folded sides up. Glue one joiner, B, beneath and one inside as shown in the top picture.

4. Glue one side of the spar just inside one inner wing, C, as shown in the middle picture. Have the sides of the spar pointing away from the fold of the inner wing.

5. Glue the top edge of the inner wing down onto the spar, keeping the bottom surface of the wing flat. Glue the other inner wing to the other spar in the same way.

Folds

Only use a little glue or the paper will wrinkle.

Add tape

Curved top

Flat bottom

6. Glue one outer wing, D, to one inner wing, matching the folds. Then glue the other outer wing to the other side in the same way.

7. Put some dots of glue along the bottom edge of the outer wing. Stick the top edge down. The bottom of the wing should be flat; the top curved.

8. Bend the front corner of each wing down along the dotted line to strengthen it. Add tape to join the two wings in the middle.

89

To make the tail and tail fin

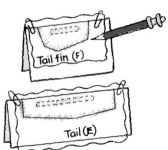

Guidelines

Guidelines

9. Copy templates E and F (the white templates shown inside template D) onto normal folded paper.

10. Trim the drinking straw to 17cm (6½in). Stick it inside the tail, E, along the guidelines marked.

11. Put some glue on the bottom edge of the tail. Stick the top edge down, keeping the bottom edge flat as you did for the wings.

12. Use a 4.5cm (2¾in) straw for the tail fin, F. Glue it inside, along the guidelines, as you did for the tail.

To make the fuselage

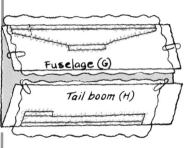

Tabs

Tabs

Diamond-shaped tube

14. Copy templates G and H onto thin cardboard. Score the blue lines firmly on both pieces.

15. Fold the sides up along the score lines on both pieces using a book and ruler (see the tip on page 88). It should make a diamond-shaped tube. Fold the tabs out on both pieces as shown.

16. Use a sharp pencil or pin to pierce a hole carefully in the fuselage, G, where it is marked X.

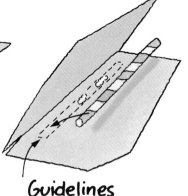

2cm(1in)

Back edge

Corner

Bottom edges

13. Glue about 2cm (1in) together along the back edge to make the rudder. Leave the bottom edges and corner open.

The back is the narrowest end.

Front

Glue as far as this line.

Have the hook pointing to the back.

The tail boom goes inside to this line.

Add glue here.

Bend a paper-clip into a hook, tape it and then stick it inside the fuselage as you did for the sky rocket on page 84.

17. Glue the top of the fuselage, G, together as far as the dotted line. Glue the top of the tail boom, H, together too.

18. Glue the tail boom, H inside the fuselage, G. The end of H should meet the line you glued up to on G, in the last step.

Now you have the finished fuselage, wings and tail. It tells you how to join them all on the next page.

To finish Superglider

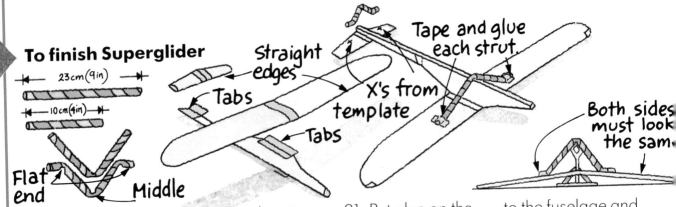

23cm (9in)

10cm (4in)

Flat end

Middle

Straight edges

Tabs

Tabs

Tape and glue each strut.

X's from template

Both sides must look the sam.

19. You need two straws: one 23cm (9in) long; the other 10cm (4in). Bend both in half to find the middle. Bend back and flatten a small bit at each end.

20. Glue the wings and tail onto the tabs at the front and back of the fuselage. Have the straight edges of the tail and wings facing forwards.

21. Put glue on the middle and ends of the long straw. Turn the plane over carefully. Check that the wings are level, then stick the middle of the straw

to the fuselage and the ends to the crosses on each wing. Add tape. Glue and tape the short straw to the tail in the same way.

Have the rudder at the back.

Squeeze plasticine into the nose.

22. The tail fin goes just in front of the tail. Glue the open edges to either side of the fuselage. Add plasticine to the nose.

23. Put a finger under each wing, by the strut, and balance the plane. If it tips backwards, add plasticine; if it tips forwards, take some away.

Flight tips

Launch it by hand first to check that it flies straight. Then try a super launch, see page 85.

Pull the glider back very gently. If you launch it too fast it will stall and crash.

To steer, bend the back of the tail fin gently to one side.

Stall

This launch is too fast.

This is a good launch – high and gentle.

92

Templates

For lots of the models in this part of the book, you need to trace the templates (outline shapes) on the next pages.

Notice that the blue line changes angle here.

V jet

Use normal paper.

Place on fold.

How to trace a template

Keep the paper in place with paper-clips.

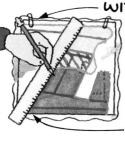

Use a ruler to trace straight lines.

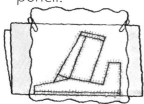

1. Lay a piece of tracing paper over the template you want to use. Trace the outline with a pencil.

2. Turn the tracing over. Scribble over the outline with a soft pencil. Turn the tracing over again.

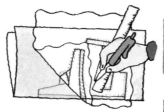

3. Lay the tracing over your paper. If there is an edge marked 'place on fold', use folded paper and place this edge on the fold.

4. Go over the traced lines again with a sharp pencil or ball point pen. Press hard so that a line appears on the paper beneath.

Tip

Lines shown in red are ones you have to cut along once you have copied the template.

Lines shown in blue are ones you have to score, once you have copied the template.

Thick lines show you which edge to put on the fold of your paper.

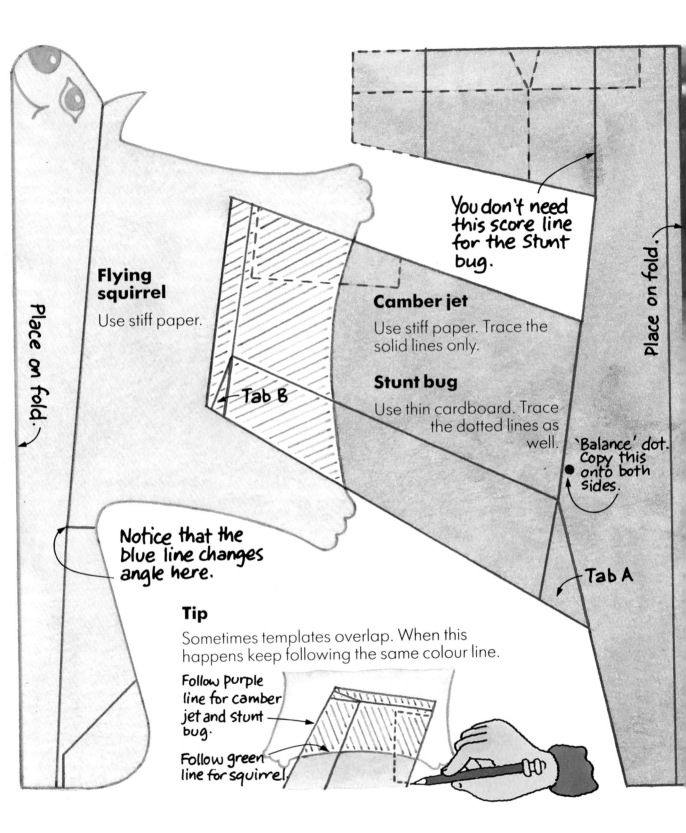

Place on fold.

Flying squirrel

Use stiff paper.

Tab B

Notice that the blue line changes angle here.

You don't need this score line for the Stunt bug.

Place on fold.

Camber jet

Use stiff paper. Trace the solid lines only.

Stunt bug

Use thin cardboard. Trace the dotted lines as well.

'Balance' dot. Copy this onto both sides.

Tab A

Tip

Sometimes templates overlap. When this happens keep following the same colour line.

Follow purple line for camber jet and stunt bug.

Follow green line for squirrel.

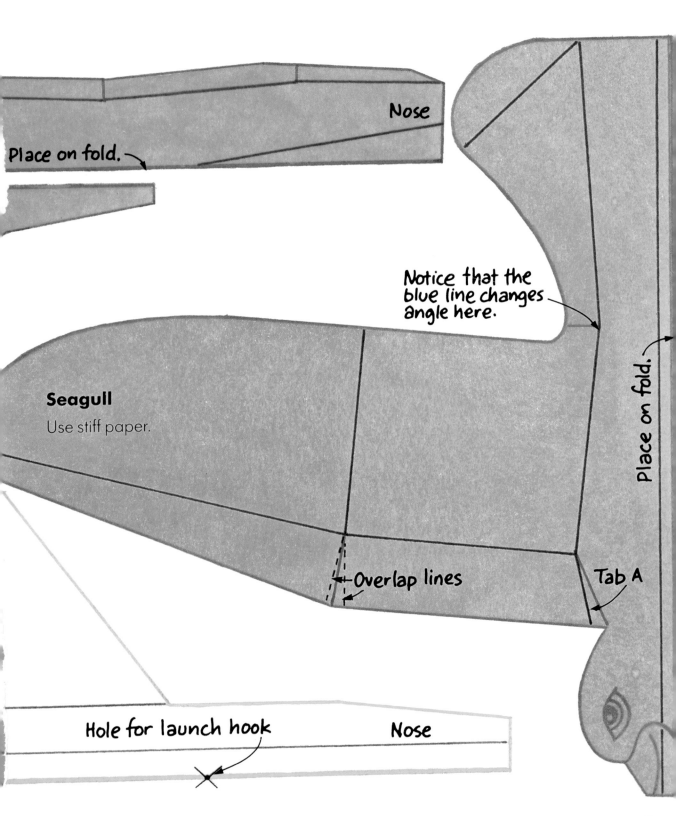

Nose

Place on fold.

Notice that the
blue line changes
angle here.

Seagull

Use stiff paper.

Place on fold.

←Overlap lines

Tab A

Hole for launch hook

Nose

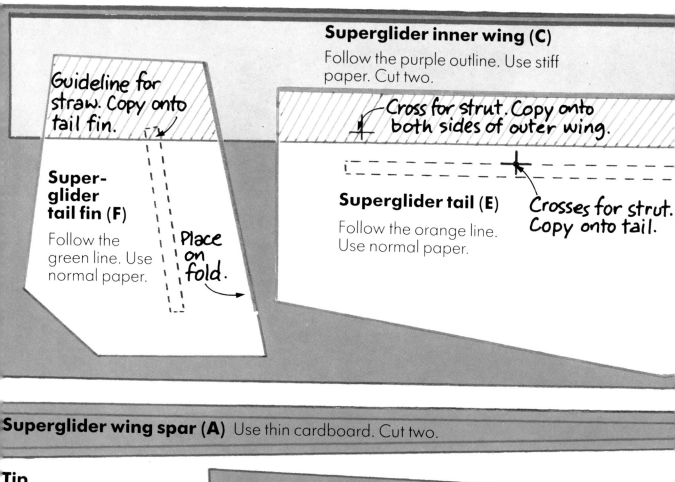

Guideline for straw. Copy onto tail fin.

Superglider inner wing (C)
Follow the purple outline. Use stiff paper. Cut two.

Cross for strut. Copy onto both sides of outer wing.

Super-glider tail fin (F)
Follow the green line. Use normal paper.

Place on fold.

Superglider tail (E)
Follow the orange line. Use normal paper.

Crosses for strut. Copy onto tail.

Superglider wing spar (A) Use thin cardboard. Cut two.

Tip

Templates C, E and F of Superglider are all shown inside template D. Make sure you follow one colour only for each template.

Superglider tail boom (H)
Use thin cardboard.

Superglider fuselage (G)
Use thin cardboard.

Hole for launch hook

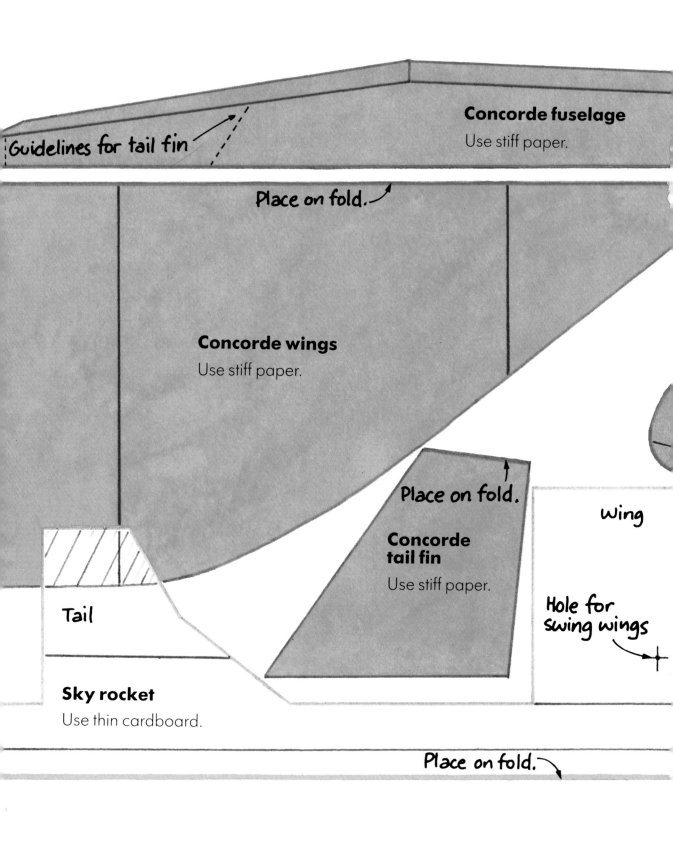

Guidelines for tail fin

Concorde fuselage
Use stiff paper.

Place on fold.

Concorde wings
Use stiff paper.

Place on fold.

Concorde tail fin
Use stiff paper.

Wing

Hole for swing wings

Tail

Sky rocket
Use thin cardboard.

Place on fold.

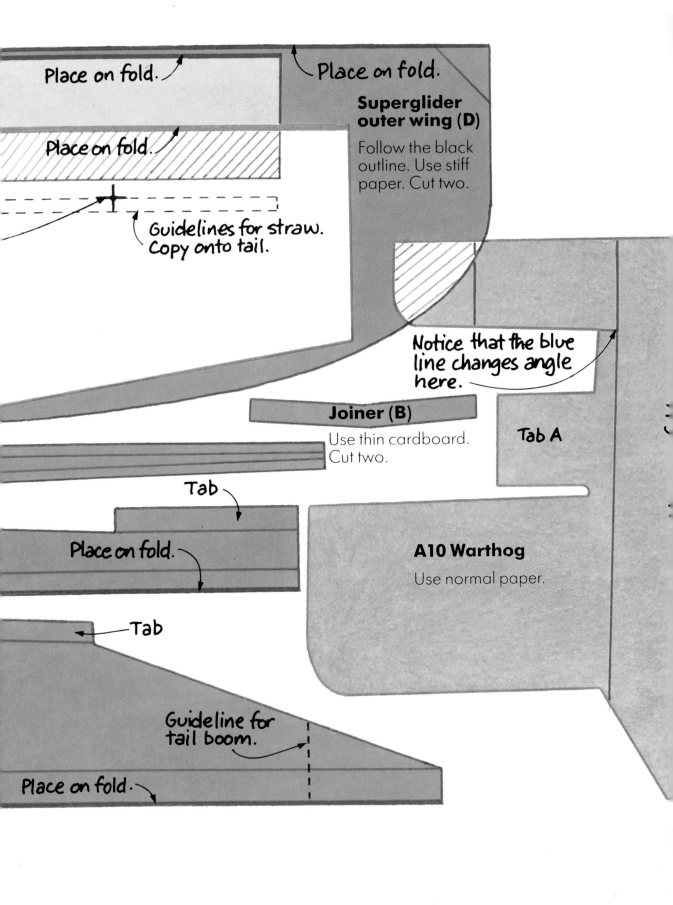

Place on fold.

Place on fold.

Superglider outer wing (D)

Follow the black outline. Use stiff paper. Cut two.

Place on fold.

Guidelines for straw. Copy onto tail.

Notice that the blue line changes angle here.

Joiner (B)

Use thin cardboard. Cut two.

Tab A

Tab

Place on fold.

A10 Warthog

Use normal paper.

Tab

Guideline for tail boom.

Place on fold.